The
Hidden
Kingdom

Ian Beck

The Hidden Kingdom

OXFORD
UNIVERSITY PRESS

OXFORD
UNIVERSITY PRESS

Great Clarendon Street, Oxford OX2 6DP

Oxford University Press is a department of the University of Oxford.
It furthers the University's objective of excellence in research, scholarship,
and education by publishing worldwide in

Oxford   New York

Auckland   Cape Town   Dar es Salaam   Hong Kong   Karachi
Kuala Lumpur   Madrid   Melbourne   Mexico City   Nairobi
New Delhi   Shanghai   Taipei   Toronto

With offices in

Argentina   Austria   Brazil   Chile   Czech Republic   France   Greece
Guatemala   Hungary   Italy   Japan   Poland   Portugal   Singapore
South Korea   Switzerland   Thailand   Turkey   Ukraine   Vietnam

Oxford is a registered trade mark of Oxford University Press
in the UK and in certain other countries

British Library Cataloguing in Publication Data
Data available

ISBN: 978-0-19-275563-6
1 3 5 7 9 10 8 6 4 2

Printed in Great Britain

Paper used in the production of this book is a natural,
recyclable product made from wood grown in sustainable forests.
The manufacturing process conforms to the environmental
regulations of the country of origin.

For Laurence

CONTENTS

... As the long arc of time passes over us, envious eyes and the lost and bitter souls of the damned look on in agonized fury ... and remember.

They remember the small joys of our green and mortal world. They remember the sunlight that plays through the leaves on a summer afternoon. They remember the slope of a beautiful neck and the turn of a smiling face. They remember the laughter of a child and the dappled pattern on the skin of a leopard. They remember a cool patch of light under cherry trees in blossom near running water. They remember the moon and the stars, they remember and rage at all they have lost, and remember too how much they would like to take it all back from us. This is a hunger that gnaws at them and that never goes away.

Our world edges against theirs in many places: the depths of dark mountains full of fire, and the deepest caverns beneath the sea. Destiny and the paths of time cross one another continually, and every so often a tiny crack opens between them. When that happens, a demon soul wriggles out, like a smudge, a flicker of poisonous smoke, and it comes forth from the darkness to raise a mortal army and try to take it all back for themselves.

1

It is rare for this to happen, perhaps only once in many thousands of years. It is always remembered by some, but such an event is never expected, and there are few now that still believe in the possibility—except, of course, for the Hidden Kingdom, the network that waits within every generation. Like sleepers in a cave they wait and are watchful for the summons of the light. They are the scattered sentinels, the guards of our mortal freedom, and they know that only one soul in that whole vast place may summon the light, and for that to happen the sword and the helm must be brought together and raised up by only that one pair of hands . . .

. . . Among the dark souls of the damned, down in the heat and darkness of Hades, among the seven principal demons there was once one other. It was she who sought to sustain and defend our world and the Hidden Kingdom. She was exiled by the seven remaining demons and she is free now, a bride of snow and ice. She is the white bride, and hers is a beauty like no other. When she rises up into the sky and begins her annual dance among her whirling flakes and ice crystals, she is both winter and vigilance. She can love a mortal man but must not be spoken of. Her love, when won, will be an ecstatic dance for all eternity . . .

From The Seventh Scroll

CHAPTER ONE

Osamu, the Prince

Prince Osamu woke suddenly to the howling of wolves. He stirred, and sat up just a little in the darkness, bleary-eyed. The wolves howled again. He slumped back, then sighed, and lazily stretched out his arm.

'What?' he said, his voice slurred with sleep.

Ayah shook him again and then she stood back with her head bowed.

The cloud of soft pillows around his head crackled. The pillows had been woven from fine linen. They looked as coarse as rough canvas, but were as soft as fine silk to touch. They released a delicate scent as his head moved. This was matched by lingering traces of the precious oil which had been carefully rubbed into his fine skin the night before; skin that had rarely been touched by direct sunlight.

He opened his eyes, looked up and saw his servant, Ayah. She was standing by his bed and she looked ridiculous. She was holding up an elaborate old-fashioned bronze storm lantern, and she had his hardly-worn outdoor hooded cloak, all edged and lined with wolf fur,

3

draped across her own narrow shoulders. He was aware then of vivid blue-and-white sparks of snow, spinning past the dark windows. It was long before dawn, but she had already wrenched aside the heavy curtain.

Ayah, with her head still bowed, pushed at him again, prodded him at arm's length, her face averted, as if he were something fearful and dangerous, a bombard of blasting powder that might explode in her face.

'Must dress *now*,' she said, 'there is no time.'

'What on earth—' he mumbled, but Ayah put down the lantern and dashed forward before he could finish. She pulled him roughly by his arm from the bed with surprising strength. Their shadows leapt together across the fine gold mosaics on the wall, and he tumbled pale and naked into the lantern light on the floor.

She bowed again, and her voice was half bullying, and half respectful.

'Dress, now.'

She knelt quickly, grabbed his wrist and the lantern, then straightened up and pulled him. She walked backwards, with her feet straddled on either side of him. His protesting feet pushed through the furs and animal skins scattered across the cold marble floor. He felt humiliated and ridiculous as she tugged him along. She quickly stood the lantern on a richly-lacquered cabinet next to a line of his favourite ceramic pots. The edge of the lantern hit one of the pots and sent it tumbling to the floor where it smashed into pieces. She didn't apologize, but tore the

4

cabinet drawers open, pulling each drawer further out than the last. She scattered clothes from the drawers in their silken wrappings, and threw them at him.

'Dress *now*,' she repeated, her eyes averted.

'Ayah!' he shouted finally, in a fury. 'What on earth is going on? Look at what you have done! That pot is smashed!'

Another figure swam into view in the golden nimbus of the storm lantern. Her head was not bowed. It was Ayah's daughter, Lissa, a rough girl of his own age. Her black hair was tied tightly in a long practical plait, and her face was as pale as the moon. She was dressed in tight hunting clothes, coarsely-sewn buckskins and furs, and she looked down at him, appraising him frankly. If he had not known better he would have sworn that there was real contempt in her look.

'I will have you both killed for this this . . . insult,' he whined.

Lissa pulled him roughly to his feet. He rushed to cover himself as best he could, feeling embarrassed in front of his servant and her daughter, who both seemed to be so mysteriously intent on signing their own death warrants.

'Dress,' Lissa said firmly. 'There is no time.' She grabbed a pair of quilted winter trousers, shook them free of their gold wrapping, and thrust them at him. Then she took some boots and slammed them on the floor. 'There is no time to explain,' she said, 'you must dress and come

5

with me now. Here!' She took his cloak from around her mother's shoulders and held it out for him as if he were a little child, fresh from the bath, ready to step into a warmed towel.

He stuffed himself as fast as he could into the trousers; anything to hide himself, to put himself on an equal footing with the women. Ayah knelt, quickly coaxed his pale feet into thick socks, and then pulled the soft leather hunting boots over them. He saw now that she was crying. Big tears rolled down her face. She straightened and pulled first a thick silk singlet, and then a quilted tunic over his head, and tugged it firmly in place, her eyes still streaming.

Lissa wrapped the hunting cloak about his shoulders and then pushed him forward and out through the half-open mirrored door which concealed Ayah's own discreet doorway to his chambers.

He looked back with one last hurried glance at the chaos of his normally calm and ordered room, and the deep cobalt fragments of the pot scattered across the floor. He was pushed out of the door and pulled along the narrow corridor that led behind the glass. Lissa walked in front of him and Ayah behind, as they snaked in secret parallel to the grand public corridor that he knew and used daily. Here the walls were dull, rough-cast, and gloomy, and only the wobbling amber light of the lantern picking out Lissa's boots showed the way through. He had never been in this space in all his eighteen years.

They paused at what he realized must be Ayah's own private bedchamber. A simple bed was tucked neatly into an alcove. It was draped over with heavy blankets and a thin, gaudily-patterned cheap fabric. A pair of worn leather slippers lay side by side next to the bed. This was the cramped dark space where Ayah had slept every night for most of his life. A single golden icon, an image of the prince, hung over the bed on the rough wall. Ayah took it down. She held his shoulders firmly and turned him to face her. He looked into her wet eyes, which were solemn and dark. His anger had faded now to a muddled confusion and rising fear.

'Lissa will take you now,' she said quietly. 'The time has come for you to obey her in all things—no one else can save you, only her. No one else can save us, only you. You must trust her in everything. You will never see me again. I have tended you since your birth, now all of that has ended. There is no time now to explain, you have trusted me all these years and now the time has come and you must trust her.' She pulled his neck down so that his head was level with hers. She kissed him twice, once on each cheek, her eyes streaming. 'Nice boy's beard,' she added with a fond half-smile, stroking his smooth cheek.

'Ayah,' he said, quietly, 'what the hell is all of this?'

'Go,' she said, shaking her head, 'now.'

Lissa's pale face loomed up again next to her mother's. The women exchanged a brief nod. They bowed their heads one to another, eyes closed. Ayah handed the little icon to Lissa, who tucked it into her tunic. Then Lissa pulled him away from the chamber, away from Ayah, and out further along the dark corridor.

After a minute or two of stumbling along behind her, he finally tugged himself free of Lissa's strong hand, and stood his ground. His face was flushed now with real anger. She turned and grabbed at him but he smacked her hand away dismissively. 'I will not move another inch until you tell me what's happening.'

She came close to him, her face against his face. Her green eyes were blank. She slapped him very hard. Hard across the pale and delicately nurtured royal face, and it hurt, and tears of pain, of anger, of humiliation, rolled down his cheek.

'There is no time, Your Highness,' she said, 'you must trust me. All is at an end. I have had the keeping of your immortal soul placed in my hands. It is what I am for, what I was born for. I have to take you away, you must move now or it will be too late.'

They stood together for a moment. He was puzzled, and he was angry and fearful too. To have been woken up and dragged naked out of his comfortable bed, harried and bullied, struck about the face, and insulted, his precious collection smashed and disturbed, each a crime punishable by a lingering death; and by his servant too, and, even worse, her low, rough daughter. There was a sudden huge sound, the echo and bass rumble of what was obviously a distant explosion. The walls shook and the stone floor seemed almost to ripple. Lissa's head dropped forward and she became as still as a rock, her hands at her side. Then she brought her hands up, joined palm to palm, and whispered something inaudible.

'Come,' she said quietly, and he did.

CHAPTER TWO

An Escape

She pulled him to the end of the corridor and down a narrow flight of spiral stairs. She had a sure instinct for the inner terrain, for the twists of the passageways, and the teetering steps of the hidden staircases. He had to trust her as she pulled him down and along with her. There was another distant explosion, and some kind of ancient dust was loosened from the depths and joints of the stone where it had lain undisturbed for seven centuries. It sifted down from the walls as they ran, and settled over them.

They finally reached a broad wooden door, with fancifully-shaped, rusted bronze hinges draped with cobwebs. The door seemed as old and undisturbed as the dust. A figure suddenly stepped out of the shadows. He bowed and then raised his shaven head. He reached into his tunic and pulled out a box. He looked just once at Prince Osamu. He opened the box with a key that hung on a gold chain around his neck. Avoiding eye contact, he lowered his head again, and with his arms raised he held the box out to Lissa. She took a larger golden key from inside the box and then silently and easily turned it in the ancient rusted lock on the door. It was clear that someone had oiled the lock mechanism and the hinges regularly. It was also clear that the rust and cobwebs had been left there as a feint: it had all been carefully nurtured to fool the casual or malevolent eye, to convince them that the door was ancient, stuck, and unused. The doorkeeper had carried out his task, and for the first time in seven hundred years or more the door was suddenly and easily opened wide.

The warm air was sucked out of the corridor along with the cobwebs and dust, and Lissa and Prince Osamu found themselves outside in howling wind and blinding snow.

The Prince staggered in shock. He had rarely felt such cold. They were at the extreme end of the southern wall of the palace. The snow had already built up in great drifts against the stone. It had settled on all the detailed carvings, in all the intricately detailed nooks and crevices, and it blew now horizontally across the surface. The Prince buried his face in the collar of his cape. It was too cold, surely, even for weathered huntsmen? He breathed in and the air crackled and froze in his nose and hurt him as if it were a knife. The doorkeeper bowed and handed a coarse leather bag to Lissa, and then shut the door behind them. From the outside the stone cladding of the door settled back seamlessly into the wall as if the doorway had never been there at all.

Wolves howled clear on the wind. Lissa waved the amber storm lamp, covered it with her hand, and then waved it again. There was the briefest glimpse of another lamp, further off away from the wall, the light veiled by swirling snow. They heard barking dogs. The air was lit with a flash of yellow-white light, and a second later there was another of the deep thunderous explosions.

'Come,' Lissa said, pulling him after her through the drifted snow towards where the other lamp had briefly shone.

They stumbled forward together, the Prince and the rough servant girl, with the snow blue-white and dazzling underfoot. The barking dogs were louder now, and then suddenly there they were: the sledge and the nervous dog team, at least a dozen dogs, maybe more, Prince Osamu couldn't tell. The sledge was piled up with furs and beside it stood a heavily muffled figure— a soldier, a courtier, a palace guard, it was impossible to say. Lissa pushed the Prince forward into the sledge and clambered quickly in after him, draping the furs so that they both all but disappeared under them. A large stone bottle full of hot water sat in the middle of the seat and the Prince put his hands around it.

'Go,' Lissa shouted.

The muffled figure shouted something guttural, and there was a sudden forward sensation as the dog team tore off into the icy darkness.

Shots and explosions rang out behind them, heavy

sounds, at once deep, but also crisp and percussive, and echoed around the sledge.

Lissa turned towards the Prince. Her eyelashes were already frosted over, and her tears had left frozen tracks of ice down her cheek. Her breath misted and mingled with his own in a sudden ice cloud. Prince Osamu had never been close enough to anyone before to experience their breath in his face. He could smell spices and lemon on hers, despite the cold. It was as if their breaths had chosen to join together in a strange new moment of freedom. It was at that point that he knew that his entire world order had been briskly swept away with no explanation. He had been suddenly expelled from the old, ritually maintained, hierarchy through the false cobwebbed palace door, and now he was nothing but a mewling, newborn infant, fatally exposed to the cold. And, as if in a final confirmation of the end of everything he held dear, he had been exposed to the close-up vapour clouds of his rough servant's daughter's spicy breath.

Somewhere else in the kingdom, high in the whirling skies, the white maiden had been stirred to raise her beautiful face from years of sleep. She was formed, it seemed, out of the very ice crystals themselves. Her white mantle a billowing snow cloud, her arms stretched as wide as the landscape below from horizon to horizon. Her mantle flowed around her slender form and

13

her hair was darkness itself, was the sudden absence of stars. She allowed herself to fall lower through the sky until she could watch and follow her players, and, if necessary, act.

CHAPTER THREE

Baku, the Apprentice

Baku's master, Masumi, was ready early. Baku could see him, bent over, walking up and down impatiently as he waited. As Baku climbed the path from his simple bed roll and the cramped but cosy lodgings inside the kiln house, he could see that Masumi was busily muttering to himself. Master Masumi had already put up his umbrella against the freshening snow flurries. Baku hurried on up the path. He had packed everything they might need for their journey the day before, but he had slept in later than he should. The dying kiln still held so much warmth, and it was so comforting that he had no wish to leave its side.

The sun may have crept up above the trees, but it was a stone cold morning. Snowflakes fell, the first of the winter, from a sky the colour of one of his master's finest grey Dobai glazes. The bundle, which was to be his burden for the journey, was heavy. His master had insisted on putting into it samples of all of his best pots. They were tucked in with soft packing straw and cyclamen-coloured fine tissue paper and were carried next to the soft bag with the sleeping rolls, quilts, and change of clothes. Baku's feet slipped on the wet path, so that in his hurry he nearly fell. That set Master Masumi off.

'I saw you, Baku,' he called out gruffly, nodding his head the moment he noticed him as if to confirm his worst suspicions. 'Where have you been, you young fool? And take care with that, remember what is wrapped up in there, mind how you carry my pots, and pray be careful on that path.'

'Sorry, sorry, Master Masumi sir,' Baku said, and then he nearly slipped again as he tried to bow to him from under the heavy pack.

'See, Baku, how the snow falls already. The long winter is here,' Masumi said, and he shook his head. 'We have surely left it too late to travel the country in this way, and yet I have no choice. The Prince has summoned me, and I hope this is not an ill omen for the success of our journey. We are forced to travel at the worst possible time. The forests will be full of hungry brigands, black bears and marauders, and perhaps worse, I have heard some terrible rumours.'

'Rumours, Master?' Baku said.

'Never mind that now, Baku, careless talk costs lives. My whole life's work, skill, and experience are all tied up in that one bundle,' he said sternly fixing young Baku with his gaze, and added, 'I have had the sense to leave a manifest with a description of every single pot with our local magistrate. Come on now,' he said briskly, 'no

16

dawdling, we must go. We are late enough in starting. Keep your eyes skinned and your wits about you.' He walked off ahead and carried on muttering to himself. He held his cloak tight about his neck. The moment they set off, out of the lee of the house and into the cold and freshening wind, Baku knew that he would soon miss their normal routine, and especially the heat of the big pottery kiln.

Chapter Four

A Glimpse of Heaven

Master Masumi insisted on walking ahead. Despite his age, and the increasing burden of the falling snow, his pride would not let him fall behind. The weight of the bundle slowed Baku down in any case. They were soon far from their town and heading downhill towards a flat plain along the valley of the river. Baku, too, was concerned about bears, bandits, and brigands now. He was no fighter, had never even held a sword let alone used one in anger, he was slight of build and also, he had to admit to himself, a bit of a coward. He feared they would be an easy target, the stout older man, and the skinny youth travelling together on foot. Masumi was well known in certain circles: he was a master craftsman, a potter of great skill and reputation, and his works were renowned, both for their great beauty and for their artful simplicity.

The pots Baku was carrying were very valuable to some, which was why Baku felt uneasy. At any moment they might be attacked and robbed. However, as the snow thickened and the wind strengthened they found there were few other travellers to be seen on the road.

An occasional person passed them, but they all had their heads bent down against the snow and wind, and mostly did not even acknowledge his master's greeting.

There was one bright moment on their first morning. Baku noticed two young women walking towards them. They were giggling together with their heads held close, and he saw that they were wearing fashionable clothes made of bright rich fabrics and they had on their tiny feet the most unsuitable shoes for walking in the snow. He had only seen images of such exotic women before in his master's collection of prints. Masumi stopped and bowed to them both. Baku stood rooted to the spot, like the gauche young man that he was, balancing the awkward heavy bundle of pots across his narrow back as if he were a donkey. They both smiled and nodded at Masumi, and then they walked towards Baku with their elegant little dancing steps.

When he saw them close to Baku noticed that they had perfect and beautifully painted faces. One of them stared at him frankly from under her parasol. Her cheeks were finely tinted in a pink-powdered blush, and her lips were a bright, carmine red, and when she smiled he saw her little teeth, which were even, and perfectly white. Her eyes were wide and green. They were outlined with black kohl and her eyelashes glittered and looked frosted, like the snowflakes that drifted slowly past her face. Baku had seen few young women in his short life and certainly none as beautiful as this. There was a radiance about her pale skin that turned her face into a symmetrical mask of beauty. To Baku she was as perfectly realized as the young nymphs and goddesses he had gazed at in the woodcuts and prints that his master Masumi collected.

After the women had passed by his master turned to Baku crossly. 'You can close your foolish mouth and stop drooling now, young Baku. Anyone would think you had never seen a young woman before.'

'No, Master Masumi. Well, it's true, not like them I haven't,' he said, looking after them as they walked away, the sound of their laughter ringing back to him through the cold air.

'High time you were settled down and married to a nice, hardworking, plump girl of your own,' Masumi added under his breath. 'No good can come of you gaping after every painted girl you see. With your mouth wide open like that you look like some fool carp in a pond.'

They walked all day. When the light went from the sky and evening came Baku was exhausted. They found an inn on the outskirts of the huge forest. His master knew the landlord, so a room was quickly found for them, and they settled in for the night.

The inn was warm, but crowded, and very busy. There were stranded travellers of all sorts. Some had been caught out by the sudden onset of harsh winter. Others were fugitives from something else, and there was a lot of excited whispering in corners.

Baku unpacked the bundle in the room. After he had unwrapped each one from its covering of soft cyclamen-pink tissue, he had to carefully lay the pots out on a shelf in a line of ascending order. There was one that he particularly liked. It was a small cobalt-blue pot with a lip on one side to pour from, and a dribbled glaze of a deeper blue colour which ran in free streaks and runs down the body of the pot. He put it a little further away from the others on the shelf. He liked to see it in its own space. The line of pots was laid out like this in the workshop too, each pot with its own space, each gaining equal respect from its own particular place in the hierarchy.

They had to wait their turn for a table at supper, which put master Masumi into a bad temper. He paced up and down a little away from Baku, his hands behind his back and shaking his head, while Baku mingled with the other travellers. He stopped in a shadowy area near two men who were eating at a table, and began, without thinking or appearing to, to listen in to their conversation.

'They'd lined 'em up against the walls,' the man with his back to Baku whispered, 'or some were half buried in fresh snow. Some of 'em just lay where they fell in rows along the corridors, or else they were propped up—hundreds of 'em, broken and dead bodies.'

'Were you there at the palace, then?' the other man asked, looking round just once fearfully, and failing to notice Baku in the shadows.

'No, but I had this direct from someone who was. Whether they were servants or warriors, they were all dragged from where they fell, and their dead faces, shocked, bloodied and broken, were all put on display as ordered. There were severed limbs and heads, and all had left great bloodied trails across the marble floors.'

'Terrible,' the other man said.

'Gets worse,' his companion replied, drinking from his cup of wine. '"Separate out the younger bodies, the Emissary only wants to see those," one of the soldiers said. "Burn the rest in the courtyard and do it sooner rather than later."'

'What emissary?' the other man said.

'Guess,' his companion said, lowering his voice even further. Baku saw the other man's face fall and grow visibly ashen. Something very bad was happening: who was this terrible-sounding emissary?

'So,' the man continued, 'the bodies were piled up all together in a great pyramid almost as high as the outer palace wall. Two soldiers threw casks of fine brandy from the cellars as well as that stuff they use to set arrows flaming, threw it all across them. Finally another soldier stepped forward, raised his longbow and fired a flaming arrow into the mass of bodies and the fire roared up at once and consumed them all, the dead, the trusting

22

palace faithful, and, my friend said, it lit up the frozen sky bright blue and orange, like an aurora from Hades.'

'Which is just what it was,' the other man whispered, 'if you think about it. We should keep moving, it won't take them long to start pressing people like us into their service.'

'We'll leave first thing.'

Baku went back to Masumi, who was very near the end of his patience. Luckily a waiter ushered them over to a corner table. When they were finally seated Masumi clapped his hands and ordered warmed wine. Baku was nervous now: when and how should he mention what he had just overheard?

When the wine arrived Masumi looked at the pottery bottle that it was served in with deep scorn. He held it up in his fingers, turning it this way and that with a furious expression on his face, as if the bottle had leapt up off the table and insulted him personally. Baku could see that his master's hand was shaking with fury and that he needed a drink at once before his temper got any worse. He clearly couldn't say anything yet. He took the bottle from Masumi's hand and quickly poured him a steaming cup.

'Here, Master,' he said. 'Drink this and you will feel better.'

Masumi put back his head and downed the cup in one, then slammed it back onto the table. Baku poured him another. After two more of the cups Masumi, with

23

a gracious wave of his hand, allowed Baku to pour one for himself. It warmed him through further, and once the food was brought to the table Baku began to feel a little better. His master's temper seemed to improve just a little too. Baku had no idea how to explain what he had just overheard, and a real sense of dread now filled his heart.

'I am wondering now about those young women we saw on the road,' Masumi said, 'those two painted-up hussies that had such an unfortunate effect on your person. You surely remember them, the two that caused your silly eyes to pop out of your head as if they were on stalks, and your mouth to fall open like a miserable fish?'

Baku nodded.

'Well, they were very far from any town or palace, and I know why.' He looked across the table at his apprentice challenging him to contradict him, to reply. Baku said nothing, just gaped back at him.

'They were following the rumours. I have been hearing conversations in here, rumours,' he lowered his voice to a rough whisper, 'of a gathering army of mercenaries.' He nodded, with his mouth turned down and a sneer across his face. 'Those sorts of women go where the mercenary soldiers are. You know what that means?'

Baku swallowed off the rest of his wine in one gulp. 'I think I do, Master, I just overheard a conversation too, just over there. Two travellers were talking, they said that the palace has been sacked, and there was worse, much worse.'

24

Masumi sat up straight, as if he had been hit with a bucket of cold water; he seemed suddenly decisive, sober. 'This means it has finally happened. A terrible war is come, an invasion force bent on the destruction of everything we work for. The signs have been there for some time. This is the worst thing that could happen. It will mean grave danger to the Prince, if he is still alive, and to the whole kingdom. To all of us, my young apprentice.' He lowered his voice to a whisper. 'And it means our journey must change direction now and we must take extra care. When we get back to the room, burn the letter from the Prince.'

'Burn it, Master? Are you sure?' Baku said.

'Are you deaf as well as stupid? Of course I am sure. If what I think is happening *is* happening, then we will want no link, no connection with us and the palace.' With that his face relaxed back and his shoulders slumped and he poured himself another cup of wine.

Later Masumi had to be helped to bed. The landlord and Baku struggled to push him up the stairs. They had to squeeze past the less fortunate souls who were crowded together on the side of the staircase, all trying to sleep where they could under their quilted coats and blankets.

Baku undressed his master and laid him down on the bed. The landlord looked at the line of pots that Baku had put along the shelf among a scattering of protective straw.

25

'My master's pots,' Baku said proudly.

'I know your master,' the landlord said shaking his head. 'That bigger one would be good for peeing in,' he added with a chuckle. Then he said, 'Sorry, no offence but they seem very plain to me. And look, this one is misshapen.' He held his lantern closer to the shelf for a better look.

'That is their secret,' Baku said pointing to the little blue pot. 'The simplicity, the subtlety of the glazes, the imperfections, the muted colours, the intrusion of natural forces: that is what gives the special pots their spirit.'

'I like a nice bright cheerful pattern myself, one with some gold and some pretty naked women mixed up in it,' the landlord said dismissively and he chuckled again and winked at Baku.

'Good night to you then.'

'Good night,' Baku said.

When the landlord had gone he pulled the palace letter out from among the transit list of his master's pots. He watched the paper darken and burst into flames, watched the sooty fragments of thin parchment fly up the chimney as if on wings, like a soot demon. A bad omen?

Baku finally settled himself on the straw mattress in the corner of the room. The fire, such as it was, had burned down and the room was cooling fast. He huddled down under the cover of his quilted coat and did his best to fall asleep. He wondered what his master had meant about 'changing direction'; perhaps it was just the drink talking. But then, the moment he closed his eyes, a pair of laughing eyes swam into view. They were followed by a pair of red painted lips, and a provocative smiling mouth. He could not rid himself of the heavenly vision of the beautiful young girl on the road. He was haunted by her teasing face. As he drifted to sleep he watched her pass by, over and over, while the snowflakes drifted. She kept turning to him and smiling.

CHAPTER FIVE

Soldiers

When Master Masumi finally woke in the morning he groaned, and sat up on his bed. He hung his head low and mumbled to himself. 'Oh,' he said. 'Ow,' and, 'no,' and 'ouch,' and 'ooohh.' He had drunk too much of the wine the night before and now he was suffering.

Baku, who had been waiting nervously since dawn for him to wake, bowed to him and said, 'Master.'

'Shhhh,' Masumi said in a quiet and quavering voice. 'Fool, *whisper* to me.'

'Master,' Baku whispered, 'I shall fetch you some tea from the kitchens.'

The stairs were clear now but the way to the kitchen was blocked by a broad-shouldered warrior in full armour. He had a hooded hawk perched on his shoulder. Baku saw the landlord, cowering in his apron, gesture for Baku to come forward. He squeezed himself past the warrior, trying hard not to be noticed—but felt a metal covered hand clamp suddenly and heavily onto his shoulder so that he winced.

'Who is this?' the warrior said in a rough voice.

'An apprentice,' said the landlord, bowing and smiling as best he could. Baku was turned roughly and found himself face to face with the fierce warrior. He wore no helmet but otherwise he was dressed ready for battle. Apart from the silent hooded bird, he had a bow across his shoulders and a quiver of arrows on his back, and, of course, a sword hung at his side. He scowled at Baku from under his black eyebrows like a dark thundercloud.

'Apprentice to what?'

'Why sir,' Baku said, 'to my master, he is a potter, Master Masumi.'

'A potter you say?'

'Yes sir.'

'Why are you here?'

He caught sight of the landlord, who had a fearful expression on his face. He sensed danger. A wrong answer now might mean almost anything.

'We are travelling and he is selling his wares at markets and the like, and I carry my master's pots, I assist him as always,' Baku said, his eyes lowered, his head bowed.

'Where is your master now?'

'He is in his room upstairs nursing his head,' Baku said, 'I am to fetch him some tea.'

'Take him his tea,' the warrior said. 'Then tell your master I want to see him down here in …' and he held his five armoured fingers up close to Baku's face. 'Have you understood?'

29

'Yes, sir,' Baku said, bowing and going on through to the kitchen. The landlord made tea and put the pot on a tray with two small cups. He bowed to Baku and whispered very quietly under his breath, 'I think they are looking for spies.' Baku went quickly past the warrior again and up the stairs.

Masumi was exactly where he had left him. His head was slumped forwards, he was still moaning quietly. Baku put the tray down gently on a low table and poured him some tea. He handed him the cup and Masumi took it with a trembling hand.

'Drink it, Master,' Baku whispered, 'you will feel better.'

Baku went to the window and raised the very edge of the rattan blind. One of the landlord's dining tables had been set up outside in the bright snow. A warrior sat behind it. He was leaning forward and talking to one of the younger guests from the inn. The soldier was jabbing at the man with his finger.

'Shut out that light,' Masumi groaned, 'what do you think you are doing, you fool, are you trying to blind me?'

'No, Master,' Baku said quietly. 'There are many soldiers at the inn. I was questioned by one of them, a fierce looking warrior, a cavalry Hawk-Master I think. The landlord told me that they are looking for spies.'

'Spies,' Masumi said, suddenly alert. 'What did I tell you? I hope you burned the letter?'

'Of course, Master, last night before I slept.'

'Good, we must hide our intentions from them at all

costs.' He looked up at Baku and shook his head. Baku poured some more tea. Masumi sighed and stretched his arms out wide.

'They are interviewing some of the guests outside,' Baku said, nodding to the window.

'They are not interviewing anybody, young Baku, they are recruiting them,' Masumi said, swallowing his tea in a gulp, 'for war, for an attack. I said it before, something very bad is happening.'

'The Hawk-Master asked to see you,' Baku said nervously.

Baku followed his master downstairs. The Hawk-Master was in the kitchen now leaning near the oven, warming himself. The hawk ruffled its wings as they approached. The warrior nodded at Masumi and Masumi bowed back to him.

'What is your business?' The Hawk-Master said.

'I am Masumi, the potter. I am travelling with my trade wares and my apprentice here,' he waved his hand behind his back at Baku and he bowed again to the soldier.

'How old is he?'

'Eighteen years, I believe, Hawk-Master.'

'Why do you need him to travel with you?'

'I have a great many of my pots to carry, I am old. And he must learn all aspects of our trade: as well as the

31

carrying, there is making, and selling too, all important aspects.'

'Where do you take these pots?'

'Why, to scattered private clients, collectors, town fairs, markets . . . whoever will buy, whoever has an eye for skilled work,' Masumi said, bowing.

The Hawk-Master stepped forward and stood over Baku, his brow furrowed, his eyes glaring. Baku could hear the plates of the Hawk-Master's armour clink and rattle as he breathed. 'Fetch the pots,' he said, and then he shouted right in Baku's face, 'NOW'. The hawk on his shoulder shrieked out a piercing cry. Baku almost fell over in his rush to get back up the stairs.

Once back in the room he gathered the pots with their tissue and packing straw one by one from the mantel. He wrapped them and laid them along the bed and then bundled them together as fast and as best he could. He took the bundle down the stairs and back to the kitchen. The landlord had cleared a space on one of the tables and stood looking up at the Hawk-Master and wringing his hands in his apron. The Hawk-Master nodded at the table. Baku lowered the bundle on to the table and Masumi said tetchily, 'Careful,' and added to the Hawk-Master, 'he is a willing enough boy, but . . .'

'But?' said the Hawk-Master.

'Nothing, sir, nothing,' Masumi replied.

Baku untied the blue-checked cloth and took out the

pots and exposed them one by one in a line across the table.

The Hawk-Master peered at them. He picked up the pots one by one and turned each of them over and shook them above the table as if he were perhaps expecting papers, or secret messages to fall out.

Masumi looked up to heaven and shook his head.

The Hawk-Master spent a minute or two studying the line of pots in silence with a look of solemn distaste on his face. 'What else are you travelling with, any other bags?'

'Just our personal things,' Masumi said.

'Bring them here.'

Baku dashed up to the room and grabbed Masumi's travel bag. He quickly pulled it open and rummaged inside for any evidence of the palace letter: there was nothing but clothes, some coins and notes, shaping sticks, and the old pierced and battered bronze bowl his Master used for shaping and extruding clay.

He ran back down to the kitchen and handed the bag over to the Hawk-Master, who tipped the contents out across the table. The clothes and coins and the little bundle of hardwood clay shapers fell out together, the bronze dish fell with a ringing clang onto the stone flags of the kitchen floor. The Hawk-Master picked it up.

'What's this?' he said.

'A vessel used in my making process,' Masumi said nervously. The Hawk-Master turned the old dish in his

33

hands, and put his armoured finger through one of the two holes in the side, 'not much use like this, is it?' he said, looking directly at Masumi.

Masumi stared back at him, suddenly silenced. Baku could see his master's gnarled old fingers working furiously as if he were moulding a piece of wet clay in explanation.

'Well?' the Hawk-Master said, taking a step forward.

'Sometimes,' Baku said quickly, 'the master must extrude coils of clay, and those old holes are the right size for the shapes of clay that he uses.'

'Really?' the Hawk-Master said turning the pitted bowl round in his hands, peering at it closely as if it might suddenly come to life in his hands. He looked back at Masumi. 'What are you looking so worried about?' he said. 'Are you trying to hide something from me?'

'No,' said Masumi, 'no, sir, nothing at all'.

The Hawk-Master put the old bowl onto the table and then picked up the bag and shook it out hard. A few hardened little balls of clay scattered over the table and a fragment of paper spun down slowly and landed among the clothes. The Hawk-Master picked up the piece of paper and turned it over.

Masumi gasped involuntarily as the Hawk-Master laid the piece of paper face up in a clear space on the table. It was a small section cut from a woodblock print and it showed a beautiful girl's face framed by long black hair against a background of falling snow.

'Who is this?' The Hawk-Master said, pointing down

at the little scrap and taking another step closer to Masumi, who was surprisingly silent and flustered.

'Well?'

Baku could see that the Hawk-Master had moved his hand down on to the handle of his sword and was about to draw it.

'Sorry, sir,' said Baku reaching forward and taking up the little image, blushing in apparent embarrassment, 'an actress from the theatre, I admire her perhaps too much,' and he pocketed the little picture.

'Pathetic,' said the Hawk-Master, 'I suggest you try and find a real girl,' and he looked Baku up and down. 'I wouldn't hold your breath, though,' he added and then laughed suddenly and loudly, as did the landlord, who nodded his head up and down in agreement. Baku blushed even redder.

'Now pack all of this rubbish up,' the Hawk-Master said to Baku, flapping his mailed hand over the pots, 'and all the rest of it.'

Baku packed everything away nervously, aware of the clink and rattle of each delicate pot against its neighbours, aware of his master's terrified stare and the giggling landlord and the Hawk-Master watching him closely, just waiting for him to do something stupid. When he had finished he tied the corners of the bundle into a knot. Then he stepped back from the table, his head bowed.

The Hawk-Master turned to Masumi and said, 'Lift it.' Masumi reluctantly took the knotted bundle and

35

hefted it up off the table. The strain showed on his face at once. The tendons in his neck stood out and his skin reddened. The Hawk-Master watched him closely, as he stood there holding the heavy bundle above the table. Baku could see his master's arms trembling. The strain looked to be too great: he would drop them at any moment and they would all smash to pieces on the table. Then, Baku thought, I will no longer be needed. The Hawk-Master will recruit me at once into his army and I will have to face going into battle against our own Prince and then I will be dead and never have lived my life at all.

He put his own arms out under the bundle and took the full weight, and Master Masumi and apprentice Baku stood locked together in front of the Hawk-Master. Masumi let go, defeated, and Baku lowered the bundle carefully back onto the table. There was a series of soft almost musical clinks as the pots settled together.

The Hawk-Master looked over at Baku. 'Strong boy, eh?' he said. 'Maybe you can win over a real girl with your muscles? I don't ever want to see either of you again. If I do . . .' he drew his mailed finger across his throat, and laughed even louder.

Then he dismissed them both with a curt wave of his hand. Baku picked up the bundle of pots, bowed to the Hawk-Master and took his master's still trembling arm, and they backed out of the kitchen.

* * *

They waited nervously in the upstairs room. Baku kept watch, looking out through the gap in the blind until the soldiers moved off. They took three young men from the inn along with them. He watched them trudge unhappily away across the clean snow, leaving their lines of footprints as evidence of the direction they had taken.

'They have gone east, Master,' he said.

'Then we will walk west,' his master replied firmly.

'Won't that mean crossing the river at a wider point, Master?' Baku said.

'No matter,' Masumi said. 'We want to keep well away from that Hawk-Master and his ragtag of soldiers. You saw how he treated me—he was looking for any excuse to use his blade. They will be part of a much larger force of well-paid, savage mercenaries and they mean nothing but trouble. I fear for our young Prince Osamu, I fear for us all. The Hawk-Master is merely one of the advance guards sent ahead of the main force, he will be looking for certain things, certain valuable things. Well, I can tell you, young Baku, he has just missed one of them. And— oh!—if he only knew it.' Masumi chuckled a little into his beard.

'Master, what valuable thing was that?' Baku said. 'Was it this?' and he pulled the little print out from his tunic.

'Bless you, no, but you did well to claim it as yours, Baku, you were thinking properly for once. Perhaps my faith in you was not so misguided after all. As to what it

37

actually was, you don't need to know now, and you would never notice it in any case,' Masumi said.

'If they seek our Prince and if the war has started, then surely we should turn back to safety?' said Baku.

'No, that is the last thing we must do. There will be no place of safety. He will have gone off and into hiding. I must find my client the Prince with more urgency than ever now.'

'Why is that, Master?' Baku said.

'That also I cannot tell you. You must trust me and that is all.'

CHAPTER SIX

On The Road West

It wasn't until mid morning that Master Masumi felt well enough to set off again. He paid the landlord, and stood and talked with him for a while out of the snow in the shelter of the porch. They were the same age and, like all old men, they liked to take the world to pieces and say how much better it had been in their day. Baku stood outside balancing the bundle of pots across his back.

They finally set to walking again. Baku followed a little way behind his master. For the most part he kept his head down out of the wind. Masumi would occasionally throw remarks back to Baku over his shoulder.

'I told you that those girls meant soldiers and war, and disaster. Those painted faces, you get a nose for these things.'

And:

'That Hawk-Master might well have clapped you in irons and dragged you off to fight if I hadn't been there to protect you.'

And:

'That innkeeper had the nerve to tell me that I need to

get some nice pictures of pretty girls on my pots if I want to sell them for high prices. Fool!'

They entered a big forest. Tall pines stretched away as far as Baku could see. It was quiet under the trees, apart from their soft footfall and the occasional flight of a startled bird. Master Masumi stopped at one point and showed Baku something growing on the side of a tree.

'The sheltered side, look at this pretty moss, springy to the touch and almost blue in colour. Rare. Feel it.'

Baku came forward and felt the little tufts of moss that spread up the tree trunk on one side.

'A wounded brigand, an injured fighter who knew his stuff, would make a poultice with it. Good for wounds, cuts, arrow injuries, cures infection. You would just stumble past it never even noticing. Nature supplies, Baku, never forget it. Colours, cures, solace: everything is in nature.'

'Yes, Master,' Baku said.

'Well, take some then, my boy. Don't gawp at it, harvest it, put it in my bag here, it will dry out and, heaven knows, what with soldiers and war everywhere we might need some of it. We should take it while we can.'

Baku was only too glad to put the bundle of pots down, even for the brief moment it took for him to take the moss from the tree. Masumi gave him a silk square to wrap it in.

'That's the way, gently now, put it in my bag carefully. You see, nature provides.'

Baku did as he was asked. Then he hoisted the pots onto his back again and they carried on. Masumi held forth for a while on the beauties and provisions of nature. Struggling with the weight of the pots, Baku hardly noticed much of what his master was saying. He was aware now only of the growing darkness, and he could sense that they were somewhere near a river— he was sure he could hear rushing water somewhere up ahead beyond the trees.

They carried on walking, or, in Baku's case, stumbling, through the cold darkness. Baku was sure at one point that he heard wolves howling somewhere from inside the deep forest, but he was too exhausted to care by the time they reached the river.

It was in full spate, the water running noisily across the rocks, and the snow was falling again and settling around them in great drifts. He was frozen and more than exhausted.

His master pretended otherwise. 'Come on, Baku, brace up, you are like all of your generation, you are weak, you have no stamina.' But it was the master who looked tired and unwell, Baku could see his hands trembling in the cold.

'I know of a ferryman's house. It should be near,' Masumi said, gesturing with his shaking hand to a spot further up the river bank. 'We need to cross the river

41

tonight, so we must go at once and chivvy him out.'

Baku stood swaying on his feet looking blankly back at his master.

'What are you waiting for, you fool? Come on.'

'Sorry, Master. Yes, Master,' Baku said, as they set off in the snow.

At the land end of a small wooden jetty they found the ferryman's hut. Baku sighed with relief as he finally put down the bundle of pots. He went and banged on the door. There was no answer. He scraped frost from the bottle-glass window and peered in, but the little house was in darkness. He walked out right to the end of the jetty. There was no sign of a ferry boat. He went back to the house and tested the door. It opened and he went inside. The remains of a fire still glowed in the iron stove. He stood for a moment in the simple room, basking in that little trace of warmth and the sudden lack of wind. He wanted to lie down at once and sleep.

He went back to the door and found a torn fragment of scroll parchment with writing on it tucked into the window. There would be no ferry until later the next day.

'Master,' he said, 'Master Masumi, sir, there is no ferry or ferryman until later tomorrow.'

'What are you waiting for, then? Let us at least go in and get warm.'

CHAPTER SEVEN

A Night Story

The ferryman's hut was small but there was a straw mattress on the floor. Masumi made Baku rummage among the shelves for something to eat. Baku found a stone jar of pickled fish and some cooked rice in a pot. He banked up the stove fire with logs from the fire bucket and set to making supper.

'Suppose the ferryman returns, Master?' he said.

'Then obviously I will pay him for food and lodging and for his trouble.' Masumi patted his own travel bag where he kept his money, the inventory of the pots, and other things. 'Stop worrying your young head and get on with it.'

They ate huddled close to the fire while the winter winds howled and screamed all around outside.

'The wind tonight sounds like the souls of all the dead on their way to the cave of Hades,' said Masumi. 'Or perhaps,' and here he fixed Baku with a serious stare, 'they are all coming out.'

'That is a terrifying thought, Master,' Baku said.

'More terrifying than you realize,' Masumi said.

For Baku it was relief enough not to be walking through the snow. He felt almost warm for the first time since they had left the inn. The pickled fish was good, and there was enough to fill him at least, but then he was all skin and bone. His master would need something more.

Baku found some wine and warmed it. After a few cups Masumi visibly relaxed. He settled back, rested his head against the edge of the mattress, and became expansive.

'That picture you found and claimed, the one the Hawk-Master shook out of my travel bag.'

'Yes, Master,' Baku said.

'I want to explain to you why it was there.'

'No need, Master, really,' Baku said, embarrassed for his old master.

'No, but I need to, Baku. You see, I too was young and foolish once, just like you. When I was myself an apprentice—and I was an apprentice in more than my craft, but I will not and cannot speak of that—I pursued beauty, Baku, real beauty. I lived for beauty. I craved it with every inch, and every fibre of my being. I fell in love with almost every girl I saw by chance in the street. I was wild with my love of beauty. I was drunk on the demon of beauty.' Masumi looked up as he said this, his eyes barely focused on Baku, and his head wobbled from side to side on his neck.

'I am sure, Master,' Baku said.

'I too had a master then,' Masumi said. 'He despaired

44

of me. One day he introduced me to a young woman. She was of good family. All of this was forty or so years ago in the old glory days, Baku. This girl calmed me down a little. She was steady, and virtuous, and above all careful with money. My master thought she would be a good match for a young craftsman, that she would ground me to the earth. Would stop me from trying, in my master's words to, "walk to the moon". And so we became betrothed. However, my eyes, these very same eyes, young Baku, they still wandered after beauty. My betrothed went away to visit her parents in a distant town. I went out carousing with some other apprentices. I remember it perfectly, it was a warm summer night with a clear sky, and in that sky every star was visible, every single star.'

'Sounds lovely, Master,' Baku said.

'It was one of those nights, Baku, when everything seems to be in place, when the mysterious gods who work our universe have moved everything to be in your favour, and, believe me, you had better recognize that time when and if it happens to you.'

'Yes, Master Masumi, sir,' Baku said.

'On the street I passed a girl. Her beauty attracted me. No, better to say it overwhelmed me, young Baku. I made a feeble excuse and broke away from my fellow apprentices and I followed this girl. After a few moments she became aware of me following her. She stopped on the wooden pathway. She stayed still, she did not turn round. I was aware only of the back of her head and of

45

her hair, tightly piled up. I was aware then of each of the tiny individual strands of her hair which were being very gently blown by the summer breeze so that each strand of hair seemed to kiss the nape of her neck. I was aware that at that moment all I wanted to do was to kiss that slender neck too. I would have willingly given up everything in my life to be allowed such a kiss. I stood still just behind her, and the busy people pushed past us without a glance or a thought, like water tumbling over two rocks in a river.'

'Like outside, now, Master,' Baku said, aware of the rushing river waters.

'It was nothing like outside now, young Baku, nothing at all. The night was warm; it was as if the very air, the stirred breeze itself caressed your skin, it felt so good to be alive. I was young and unaware of my body and all its youthful perfection, I paid it no heed I just *was*. I drank wine, I pursued young women, without a care in the world.' He stopped and lowered his head, looked down at his empty bowl and fell silent.

'What is it, Master?' Baku said.

'I fear I will betray, will hurt,' he said quietly with a catch in his voice, almost a sob.

Baku did not know what to say in reply. They sat together for a long moment in silence. He had the idea that his master might have been crying, although his head was held so low that it was hard to tell. He poured a little more of the warmed wine and pushed the cup across to Master Masumi. He took it in his fingers, fingers that could shape clay to his will, fingers that could mould and caress and perfect. Baku watched as Masumi idly stroked the sides of the ferryman's humble cup. His fingers probed the cup as if it were something he had made himself and was testing for flaws. He examined the cup as if he were a blind person. Baku felt the displaced emotion that Masumi was pouring into the humble fired clay. Masumi held the cup up into the lamplight. He turned it round in his fingers. The warm wine steamed, and when Baku looked into his master's eyes he saw that they were dry, without even the trace of a tear.

Masumi drank the wine off in one. He slammed the cup back onto the floor with a bang.

'Time to sleep,' he said brusquely.

'But, Master,' Baku said, 'the girl in the street, that summer night, what happened?'

Masumi looked at Baku and smiled and shook his head. 'You want to hear the end of my story then, my young Baku.' And he laughed then, a hacking old man's laugh, throaty and growling, and shook his head. He held the cup out and Baku filled it up again.

'I walked past the girl. I walked past her very slowly and then I turned back to face her. She stood there on that wooden sidewalk perfectly still, perhaps as far away from me as you are now.' Masumi reached his hand out and touched Baku. 'That close,' he said, and put his hand on Baku's shoulder. 'We looked into each other's eyes.

It seemed it was for a long time, an eternity. You know, Baku, sometimes I feel I am still looking into those eyes, right now at this moment, that my life has never moved on from that night, not for one second.'

'It sounds as if you are haunted by her, Master.'

'You are more right than you know. It is just that, Baku. In truth it must have been only for a second. At that same moment our hands reached out towards one another. I took her hands in mine and her face broke into a smile. She pulled me forward and she whispered just one word to me: "Run," and we did, we ran through the summer night, down the side streets until we reached the river. We stood by the water under the stars. We were young, Baku, and I felt eternal; as if I were a god and she was a goddess, drawn down from the skies, from the constellations. I kissed her and her mouth was cool to my lips and she yielded to me at once. I had never felt kisses like that.'

It was then that Baku saw the tears fall from his master's eyes, in shining lines down his cheeks. Masumi fell silent again. This time he did not break his silence. He just stared past his apprentice, lost in his thoughts.

Baku took the cup from him and helped him up. His master stood in silence and watched Baku as he laid out the bed roll on the mattress and moved it nearer to the fire.

'Here,' Baku said, 'sleep, Master Masumi, sir, rest.'

Masumi remained quiet, and sat for a while on his bed roll.

'I loved that girl,' he said quietly, 'I loved her just that once, and that once was for ever, for eternity. Now I have betrayed her. I have no courage at all. I have never told anyone about that girl, that woman, that haunting ghost until now, at this moment. That little picture that I hid in my bag is the closest image that I ever found to help remind me of her beauty. I shouldn't have said a word or admitted even that, because, you see, it will be the end of me . . .'

'You must not upset yourself, Master,' Baku said. 'It was a long time ago, you were young. You must get some sleep now, it has been a long day.'

'Are the pots safe?'

'Yes, Master.'

'Is my bag safe?'

'Yes, Master.'

'Promise me, whatever happens, to look after the travel bag, too. It's very important and everything in it is important, even down to the very humblest thing.'

'Of course, Master. Come on, rest.'

Masumi lay down heavily and slowly tucked himself into his bed roll, with his head as close to the dwindling fire as he could get.

'Build the fire up, Baku,' he said, and added, 'Be a good maker and tell no one of what I said, about the woman.'

Baku added a log from the bucket. He blew out the lamp and bundled himself into his own bed roll. He lay in the cold trying to warm himself, and before long he heard his master's snores, which sounded like an old bull-frog on a lily pad. He thought of his master as a young man, perhaps of his own age, embracing the beautiful young woman near the river, and then he thought about the beautiful girls they had seen on the road. He had never experienced anything like that in his short life, and wondered if he ever would, now that a terrible war had started. He had never experienced war or fighting of any kind. He knew of it only from the scraps of history he had learned from Masumi while they worked together, from the woodcut prints of battles and fighting warriors, and from the occasional glimpse in the street of swaggering mercenary warriors for hire, in their armour. He knew vague fragments of the legends and prophecies of the recurring war, the battle with the demons. It was all a frightening blur. Who would be fighting whom, he wondered? And how could he keep himself very far out of it? Baku fell asleep then, deeply asleep, but he woke suddenly into the strange bright white light of a dream.

CHAPTER EIGHT

Baku's Dream

The ferryman's hut was filled with bright white light, or so it seemed to Baku. He sat up in the tangle of his bedding. The cabin was as cold as ice. His breath misted at once like a thick cloud in front of him. Baku's face and head felt tightly stretched and his scalp tingled with pain, it was so cold. He blinked and screwed up his eyes at the source of the light.

A beautiful girl, a maiden in white robes, stood in the room between him and his master. Her face was as white as the snow outside, almost as white as the dazzling white light that surrounded her. Her dark eyes looked at Baku intensely. She raised a fine pale finger to her lips, lips the colour of blood. Baku remained still and watched her. She bent over the sleeping figure of his master. She appeared to kiss him on his mouth. She was surely the dream of the love of Masumi's life come back to him again, after all this time. Baku smiled with dream pleasure for his master. How delighted he will be, he thought, when he wakes and finds her here. She lifted her red lips from Masumi's face and opened her mouth wide. A stream of ice-white smoke seemed to pour from her and enter his master through his mouth. It was a long stream of smoke and it seemed as if she were blowing something cold but vital into him, and all the time her beautiful eyes were fixed on Baku. The stream of white smoke seemed to go on for a long time, as is the way with dreams. Baku watched, fascinated, aware that he was dreaming, but still taking part in the dream. He enjoyed seeing the beautiful maiden of his master's youth conjured before him, as in the story, everything clear, and all of it seemingly conjured from a jar of pickled fish and some wine in a ferryman's hut.

Finally the stream of bright white smoke stopped. The girl lifted her head, shook her raven-black hair, which was worn loose and long and trailed down her white mantle. She walked towards Baku, and it was as if she were floating across the space between them, so light did she seem.

'My master will be so pleased to see you,' Baku said to her, thinking to himself, 'I am a fool, to speak to a dream.'

The girl bent towards Baku and then spoke in a musical and delightful voice. 'You must promise me something.'

'Anything,' he said, smiling up at the radiant girl.

'You must promise me that you will never speak of me in the way that he just did.'

'You must wake my master,' Baku said, 'he will be so very happy that you have come back to him.'

'I cannot wake him. You must promise me,' she said again.

'Of course I promise,' Baku said, smiling at the dream girl.

She came closer to him and he stared, mesmerized by her beauty and by the radiance, the light that shimmered around her. She laid her finger upon his lips, and he would later swear that he actually felt the cool and very real pressure of that dream finger sealing his mouth. 'You must promise me another thing: that whatever happens, and no matter how far, impossible, or dangerous it seems, that you will find the Prince. I will be with you now always, and I will help when I can. But remember you must not speak of me.'

'I promise,' he mumbled. His eyelids felt heavy, he shivered all over and then fell back to sleep at once, into the cold darkness, into the fug of his bed roll, and he dreamed no more.

CHAPTER NINE

A Long Walk in the Snow

When Baku woke it was already daylight. He had no idea of the time, but, judging from the light streaming in through the windows, it was time to be up. He got up from his bed roll and cleared it away at once. He rolled and tied the ribbons. He put them in the bundle and checked the pots, all were safe. Master Masumi was still fast asleep. The hut was freezing cold, and so was he. The fire was nothing but white ash. He took the wine cups outside. The snow had deepened, and it was still snowing yet. He leaned over from the wooden jetty and rinsed the cups out in the rushing waters of the river. The water burned his fingers it was so cold. He hurried back into the hut, taking care to shut the door quietly so as not to wake his master. He tidied away the cups and did his best to make the squalid hut presentable. They would have to leave soon, and 'arrive' again once the ferryman had returned, and then they could cross the river and enjoy a good breakfast at the inn. The waters, though, were still in full spate. He wondered, looking through the window, whether a simple ferry could cope with such rapids. It was time to wake his master.

Masumi looked at peace, and Baku hardly dared to disturb him. He leaned over and shook his master's shoulder very lightly. Masumi did not stir. Baku pushed at his shoulder again, more vigorously: nothing. Still Masumi did not stir. A shiver of fear and panic went through Baku as fast as the river water. He trembled, and felt his hands shaking. He touched Masumi's face. It was as cold as the river, as cold as he felt, and as still as a stone. He pulled down the bed covering and put his ear to his master's chest. A cold silence, nothing. He couldn't even hear the echo and thump of his own heart, which he was sure would be racing in panic. His master, Masumi, the great potter, was clearly dead.

DEAD.

There was no one to turn to for help. How was Baku to explain his death? What of the authorities, the constable, the magistrate, the soldiers, even the ferryman who would surely be here at any moment? How to tell him that there was a dead man in his hut? He sat down next to his master and wept.

Baku soon pulled himself together. He was filled with guilt and, for some reason, he was certain, in his muddled panic, that he would now have to erase all trace of their visit, to make it seem that they had never been there at all.

He opened the door of the hut and propped it open, and noticed even now that the snow began to drift in through the door and onto the mat. He pulled his master out by his feet and laid him in the snow. The body sank comfortably back into the crisp whiteness as if Masumi were back lying in his bed at home. Baku went in and fetched out the bed roll and the bundle of pots and his master's travel bag. He took his own bed roll out from among the pots, tied up the bundle again and took the wrapped pots out further into the snow. He went back into the hut and found a shovel near the stove. He took it out to where he had left the bundle and dug a deep hole. He went to drop his master's pots into the hole and stopped himself. He laid the bundle down and opened it. He rummaged among the pink tissue, took out the little bright cobalt-blue pot and put it in his pack. He tied the bundle again, dropped it in the hole and quickly shovelled the snow back over. The snow was soft and crisp and easy to dig. He went over and pulled his master further away from the hut, pulling him by his feet into the deeper snowdrifts. He dug as deeply as he could, his heart thudding.

Then he covered Master Masumi with the snow next to his pots. He mumbled a prayer over the mound. After that he watched the snowflakes fall and cover the disturbed surface, so that within a few short minutes the old snow and his old master were covered over with a bright, fresh, white winding sheet. His master would sleep now, undisturbed, until the spring. He supposed, however, that the wolves might find him sooner rather than later, and that the evidence of his master might all be gone. He promised that, if he could, he would come back and bury him properly and rescue all the beautiful pots too. He would need to draw a map of some kind if he were to find the place again.

It was quiet outside except for the rushing river. The forest they had walked through the night before stood in silence all around him. There was no obvious place to go. He could walk back through the woods, the trees at least offered shelter of a kind, and he could get back onto one of the main routes and do his best to find the Prince, despite the wolves and the marauding soldiers. He decided to walk further on into the forest and find another place to cross the river. He went and looked inside the hut for a scrap of vellum, parchment, anything to mark. He found a scrap of parchment and a small brush and a pot of ink. He marked the hut and the river, the rocks at the bend and he even drew the outline of the building. He looked around for any last sign of their presence: not even their sour smell remained, it had all been blown out by the freezing air. He picked up the half-jar of wine. He tipped some of it into the little blue pot and stopped it up with a piece of cork, then shut the door of the ferryman's hut. He picked up his master's travel bag, even though it felt wrong now and somehow intrusive. There was at least some money left, coins and notes, and he would need them once he had found an inn. There was the old bronze bowl-shaped clay mould with the holes. He took it out of the bag and looked at it carefully. It was rusted over and covered in verdigris, and surely not much use. He walked back to where he had buried his master and was about to add the old bowl to the grave when something caught his eye, some way off under the trees. It was a swirl of white, a column of snow and ice whirling in place. He saw her face then: among the spinning flakes and crystals her eyes pierced through him and she opened her mouth.

'Take everything with you, everything in that bag,' she seemed to say. Although he heard the sound of the cold wind in the pine branches and the river water, there was her voice as well, close, intimate, a whisper in his ear.

He looked down at the mould, a dirty looking and undistinguished old bowl, the inside covered over with dried clay. His master had carried it with him, close to his person. It had meant something. Masumi had said that everything in the bag was important and now the girl seemed to have said it too, although when he looked back the column of snow had gone. It was then that he felt a slight tingle in his hands, a charge of something, an odd feeling of contained energy. He put the bowl back into the bag and tucked the folded map inside too. Without another thought, he slung the bag over his shoulder and set off back towards the dark trees of the forest. He took care to scuff over his footsteps as best he could with a branch, scattering little dark flecks of pine needles across the snow. They in turn would be covered with fresh snow, the footprints, the pots, his master, the pine needles, all of it would soon be dissolved in clean whiteness like a new page, unwritten.

He walked fast for an hour or so. He wanted to put some distance between himself and the ferryman's hut. He could walk fast because he was no longer burdened with the heavy bundle of pots. His overriding problem was that of hunger, that and his overwhelming feeling of deep cold, bone deep. He just could not get warm. Walking through the severe cold drained what little energy he might have had left after the shock of his master's death. He still could not believe it. His master, Masumi, was dead, dead of the cold or of shock. Or had the pickled fish poisoned him? He was walking among some very dark overhanging trees when he realized something, and stopped in his tracks. There was silence all around, no bird song, and the river was far enough away. There was no sound at all but the occasional thump of snow falling from branches and the creaking of the trees.

He realized that the girl, the one in his dream, his master's summer girl from the past, was the same one who had just spoken to him close in his ear. How could he have not realized before? She was so vivid, so real and palpable. He was sure that not only was she the same girl from that far-off summer of forty years before, but she was also in some way his master's death. Had he dreamed

59

his master's death? It seemed possible for a moment that he had conjured death itself in his sleep. He had also promised her things. She had touched his soul, his being. She had touched his mouth and he had gazed into her eyes and found what he believed was love there, and now he was bound to her for ever, and love and death were linked together in his heart and soul. He felt suddenly colder than ever. He walked on into the snow.

CHAPTER TEN

A Journey

Lissa felt a sudden and terrible apprehension deep inside her. It was as if her soul had been suddenly squeezed by a ruthless armoured hand. There was a wrenching feeling, and her head reeled as if she were looking down from a very high place at a distant chasm. Her stomach lurched. She involuntarily turned at once and looked back at the spinning wake of snow behind them. The wide plateau of even snow stretched back into the early darkness for miles. To her gaze the sky was a solid black on the horizon, but in her imagination, in her soul, it was lit underneath with a fierce blue and orange line which glowed upwards and then faded back to black. It is over, then, she thought, suddenly drained of energy. A sad wave of nausea coursed through her. All those lives gone, suddenly burned away, scorched ashes now and whirling grey dust. Just her and the Prince Osamu left. Once they found that he had escaped, things would get worse— they wouldn't stop looking, ever.

The wrapped and pampered Prince Osamu was beside her. His head was turned away, and his pale face

61

was part hidden in the furs that covered them both. He seemed to be asleep. He was entirely in her hands now, she was responsible for him for every second of every day for as long as it took, and she knew that could be a very long time. The dogs would surely soon flag—they could not go on for much longer—and pursuing riders might even now be following them. As long as the dogs lasted she should rest. She settled herself, turning her face away from the Prince.

Lissa woke with a start. The dog sledge had stopped. They were at the edge of a forest. The dogs were still and panting, one or two of them lying down in the powdery snow, and the rest standing in harness, their breath misting, tongues lolling. She turned and looked behind them but there was no sign of any pursuit, just the even black of the sky. The snow clouds had passed over and the stars were now clearly visible. They must have travelled and slept through the whole of the short winter day. The sledge man was nowhere to be seen. Lissa sat up straight, alarmed. She stepped down from the sledge. She pulled a short dagger from her belt and looked for any sign of the driver. His boot tracks led away into the trees. The Prince was well wrapped up and still slumped asleep under the warm layer of furs. She risked the short walk away from the sledge. The dogs were quiet. They will be tired and thirsty too, she thought. She set off into the forest. It was dark under the tree canopy but the snow reflected enough light to see a little way in. At first she saw no sign of the sledge driver. What on earth did he think he was doing, abandoning us like this? she thought.

She took a few steps further in under the trees. Then she saw him. He was sitting on the ground, slumped awkwardly against a tree. She called out to him in a harsh whisper, but he took no notice. She took another step forward, and saw the trail of red on the snow. Another step and she saw the arrows, many arrows; one had gone right through his throat, pinning him to the tree, and another had gone straight into his heart. She turned back to the sledge, warily keeping just inside the protection of the tree line. She heard the unmistakable swoosh of an arrow in the air. One of the dogs howled and fell over on its side. Another dog was hit, which set the others off barking and howling. She kept low and ran back towards the sledge; she felt the air move as something whistled past her head, and an arrow thudded into the snow safely beside her. She saw movement as the Prince finally sat up in the sledge.

'GET DOWN NOW,' she screamed, as another arrow sped past her. She turned and rolled across the snow. She saw the archer standing some way off, dressed all in white snow-camouflage. Her best hope was that there was only one of them, a lone brigand. 'Stay down,' she called out to Osamu and then she ran straight at the archer. He raised his bow and she watched him stretch back the rawhide string, and his eyes narrow and focus clearly under the fringe of white fur from his hat. She was a narrow target and faster than a bird. She leapt upwards, the knife now between her teeth, one leg straight out in front of her and one knee raised. The archer loosed an arrow at her but it glanced off the thick sole of her boot. The archer had no time to load another arrow against the string before her boot caught him across the bridge of his nose, breaking it and knocking him back onto the snow. He was strong and managed to push her off, but Lissa somersaulted in the air, dropped the knife into her hand and threw it hard. She heard it thud into his chest, and he slumped back with a gasp of steaming breath. She climbed onto his chest, pulled the bloodied dagger out with both hands and quickly sliced it hard across his exposed windpipe. Blood sprayed in an arc across her face and the brigand made harsh gurgling sounds as the life ebbed out of him.

She grabbed a handful of clean snow and wiped it across her face, cleaning off some of the blood.

'Disgusting,' said a voice behind her.

The Prince stood a little way off with his arms wrapped around himself, his head half turned away from the sight of the steaming blood splashed across the snow and the gaping wound on the brigand's throat. Lissa stood, picked up the brigand's bow, and then kicked the body over on to its face in the snow. She knelt and pulled off the quiver of arrows with a tearing wrench. She said nothing to the Prince but walked over to each of the dead dogs and putting her boot on the bodies to steady them pulled the arrows out of them too. She picked up two other arrows where they lay on the snow. Then she walked back into the trees and pulled all of the arrows out of the sledge driver too. The Prince half followed behind her, not wanting to be left on his own.

'How could you?' he said, his lip curling, sneering with distaste.

'If I hadn't, and if I couldn't, Your Majesty, then you would be dead along with the dogs, and that poor man who just gave his life to protect you.' She slung the quiver and the bow across her back. 'Useful weapons,' she said. 'Now, if you would, count how many of our dogs are left.'

'I will not take orders from you.'

'We have no time, so you have to. He may have been one of a dozen brigands out looting on this road; or he may have been part of a search party looking for us and the others may find us at any moment, and that will be the end of us and the end of everything. Now, count the dogs . . . *Sire!*'

He turned his back on her, away from the sight of the dead driver and of her own smeared and bloodied face. He stood silent and shivering as the remaining dogs growled and barked. He would not give in. She must count the dogs. He was trembling, and not just from cold. He was deeply frightened.

'Three dogs left,' she said, 'not enough to pull us. I

should kill them just to spare them from any more suffering.' She stood over the remaining dogs still tethered to their dead companions. She held her knife out in front of her and approached the first dog. It looked up at her and made a low whining sound in its throat. Lissa moved forward and knelt close to the dog.

'No,' said the Prince, and in horror he watched her knife arm cross the dog's throat. The dog yelped and moved away. Lissa had simply cut through the holding reins. She clapped her hands and the dog barked, ran off a few paces across the snow and looked back at her. She threw some snow at the dog and it ran off further towards the trees. She cut through the reins of the other two dogs and shooed them away too. She quickly rifled through the contents of the sledge and the seat box. She took a shoulder bag and filled it with some scraps of food, the sledge man's pistol and some bullets, and draped it over her shoulder.

'Come on,' she said. 'We will need to find shelter, and soon.' She walked off without a backward glance at the Prince. The dogs scattered away from her further in among the trees.

She stopped and turned. The Prince was standing with his back to her. She looked down at the blue-white ground, felt the cold and the keening wind knifing through the layers of skin and fur. All her life she knew that this moment might come and now it was here. The Prince Osamu was her calling, her responsibility. For him, she had been trained from birth—years of servitude. And he had apparently rejected it all. It seemed that from the height of his ivory tower he saw her as someone beneath contempt. Here they were out in the snow and darkness, surrounded by blood and dead dogs. His disgust could not be more obvious. She had heard the rumours at the palace that the Prince cared nothing for battle training, that he had no belief in the old prophecies, and the teachings of myth and legend. That was all it was to him, quaint mythology.

She had a choice in front of her. She remembered the tear-stained face of her mother, and felt the icon of the Prince still tucked in her bodice. Her duty had always been clear, her life for the Prince's. Now she saw another possibility, she might slip away into the darkness and leave the Prince to fend for himself. There was a path through the forest ahead, a path to freedom and survival and a new life. She looked back at him: he was still standing sulkily with his back to her, surrounded by the scattered dead dogs, his arms wrapped fiercely around his body as if he were hugging himself. She adjusted the bag across her shoulder and, ignoring the Prince, went over to the body of the brigand and stripped his bloodied sheepskin coat from his body, rolled it up and stuffed it into the travel bag. Something else caught her eye, the glint of the handle of a sword. It was tucked in a dark scabbard and she hadn't noticed it before. She unbuckled it and tucked it into her waistband. She walked over to the Prince. No

67

more thinking, no more hesitation.

'Come,' she said and pulled at him. He spun round and faced her, trembling and blazing with anger and fear.

'I will have you killed. All that has happened to me today will lead to your certain death, you should die just for slapping me. I am the Prince Osamu and I will have you executed. Your mother too.' His voice quietened and then stopped, and his arms fell to his sides. His pale, delicate face stared out at her from under the hood of his cloak.

'You are no longer the Prince. You can never refer to yourself as the Prince. All of that is over. We must move away from here and go now. We have far to travel. There will come a time when I can tell you why, but this is not the time. We need to get to the plains far from the river and beyond the forest lands. That is where the prophecy leads; that is where it will all happen. It is enough to say to you that certain signs have come to pass—you should surely understand that.'

'I understand that you are in a misguided thrall to all of that old religious prophecy, just like my tutors.'

They stared at one another in the cold gloom under the trees.

'Whatever else you believe, Majesty, you can surely see that I have certain skills. You may despise them, but they will keep you alive. We are on foot now. Come into the forest with me. You must trust me as my mother said. By the way, you cannot have my mother killed: I am sure she is already dead, and killed by the same forces that want *you* dead most of all. Now, come on.' She turned on her heel and headed back to the tree line fast, without looking back at the Prince. It was now or never. He would have to follow her or die.

CHAPTER ELEVEN

Shelter

Baku knew that he had to find shelter, and very soon. He was walking through the heavy drifting snow in a kind of numbed daze, a dream, a nightmare of cold. At first he thought he was imagining or remembering her, the beautiful woman the ice maiden, but then he realized that he was really seeing the pale, white-robed maiden of death quite near him while he walked. Her robes were whiter even than the snow, and she seemed to float above the ground: he could not see her feet and she left no footprints. She was leading him in a specific direction and he followed her with no idea of how long or how far it would take him. He was both fascinated by her beauty and, at the same time, terrified of her too. He remembered the stream of white smoke that seemed to pass from his master, Masumi, to her—or from her to Masumi, how could he tell? 'Perhaps,' he said out loud into the storm of snowflakes swirling round him, 'you are just waiting for me to collapse and then you will come over and take my soul away to Hades too. And . . . I have not even lived yet.' He shouted this last part across to her as if pleading for his life to continue for just a little longer.

'What's that you say?' an answering voice came out of the darkness, and it was not the maiden's fluting voice—it was a man's voice, a deep growling peasant's voice.

'I say that I am lost and that I have not yet lived or loved,' Baku shouted wildly back into the wind at the top of his voice, thinking he was finally mad and answering the sound of the wind. It was then that a smudge of warm-looking light swam into view off to the side where the snow maiden had just been floating. There was the shadowy shape of a low building visible through the snow and a lantern was waving in front of it.

'Over here,' came the voice again.

Baku stumbled across in the vague direction of the voice, whipping his head round, looking for the maiden in white, but she had gone.

He bumped into a man wrapped in what seemed to be layers of skins. His face was hooded over and he was holding up a storm lantern. As Baku fell into unconsciousness he heard the shriek of a circling hawk from high above and felt a strong arm grab at him, and the man's voice said, 'Come on, lad, or it'll be the end of you.'

When he opened his eyes Baku saw that he was inside a simple wooden hut. There were several sleds and toboggans of various sizes hanging on the walls. There were

71

animal skins too, stretched out on frames. There was a solid stone fireplace and a big fire with crackling sparks and the smell of woodsmoke. And sitting opposite him was the weathered smiling face of an old woodsman or huntsman, supping from a big bowl.

'Some soup for you, my cold friend, yes?'

'Yes, oh yes,' Baku said.

The huntsman put down his own steaming bowl, fetched another and gave it to Baku.

'Thank you,' Baku said, hoping to feel the warmth return to his dead fingers, as he sipped at the scalding soup. 'Oh,' he said. 'Oh . . . ouch . . . mmm, good.' Soup trailed down his chin. 'Oh, thank you,' he said again, feeling a trace of warmth coursing through him. He felt as if he had been frozen solid for weeks.

'Much longer out there tonight, my friend, much more dancing with the snow demons, and you would be with the Gods.'

'You don't know how right you are,' Baku said with a wry smile.

'Where were you going?'

'I was on a mission,' Baku said, and then immediately regretted it. The huntsman's face darkened and he scowled at Baku.

'Mission?' he said, suddenly wary and fearful. 'You are not with the invading soldiers, are you?'

'I am no soldier,' said Baku, 'nor am I a spy. I am an apprentice potter.' He regretted this too and hastily changed it. 'Well, that is I was once an apprentice, but no longer. I am a potter in my own right now.'

'Ah,' said the huntsman. 'A maker, that is always a good thing.' And he nodded and smiled, relieved. 'Only I have seen soldiers, many of them camped just outside the forest—foreigners, with wolf-fur capes and fish-scale armour. I have an idea where they are from, so I have kept well away from them. I hope they did not see me, but then usually nobody sees me unless I want them to. You are the first stranger to cross my threshold for many, many years. It is strange, but I cannot help feeling it was meant, somehow. Some instinct, some unease made me step outside just now with my lantern. It is not something I would normally do on a terrible night like this, but something compelled me to go outside, and look what happened—I saved you, my friend,' and he laughed with a low, rough chuckle.

'Yes you certainly did,' said Baku, seeing the maiden in white in his mind and turning at once to the window where he saw nothing but a flurry of swirling flakes. 'This soup is very good, by the way.'

'Caribou flesh, caribou bone stock, wild garlic, mushrooms and white onions. I waste nothing and I keep it going on the hearth, so that it lasts, and I add to it from time to time. A very sudden and harsh cold spell we are having just now. Two very bad omens: the cold and an invading foreign army. Wherever you were going I think you had best bed down here, don't you? It's not much but

73

it is warm, and look—I even have some of this.' He handed Baku a cup of warmed wine. 'To your health, young man, and also to your company, for I am always alone here, and have been for forty-five years. I am one of those leftovers from the old time,' he nodded and then drained off his wine in one.

'My master, well, my old master, my late master, always said he was from the old time too, he told me more than once that he was from the Hidden Kingdom, but he never would explain it to me. I helped him at the kiln and that seemed enough to me, but then he would say things like, "When the time is right, you will be admitted to another mystery, another training altogether." When I asked him what he meant he said that I was not yet of age, and called me a fool; he was like that.'

'A dangerous and troubled history to discuss openly, so I think your master was a wise man to keep his counsel,' the man said. 'And the very young are often headstrong and foolish, we all were once.'

There was a silence between them; a log shifted in the fire.

'I should like to propose a toast to my old master, may the gods rest him,' Baku said.

'To your old master,' the huntsman filled his cup again and drained it.

Baku held the humble little drinking cup up to his face and studied it critically as he felt sure his master Masumi would have done. The glaze was speckled in shades of

74

grey, like a bird's egg. The lip of the cup had a wavering line of dark umber glaze around the edge with some runs and dribbles of glaze streaking the body. It was a masterly little cup, artfully artless and made with a sure hand and a fine, sensitive eye.

'You are admiring my little cup?'

'It is a very simple cup but I would say that it was made by a master's hand.'

'You are an observant youth. True, it is the work of a very *old* master. I have four such cups but rarely the chance to use more than one of them, because of course I have lived here alone all these years.'

'Who made them?'

'I did once; in another life.'

'*You* made this?'

Baku sat up straight suddenly, amazed that he had been rescued from a certain and freezing death by another potter, who, it seemed, had once been the equal of his own late Master Masumi. He saw at once the possibly frightening pattern in his fate. The white maiden had surely chosen him and led him here for a purpose. He almost went to speak, to explain, but remembered he must say nothing.

'I think it surprises you that I was once a maker, like yourself or your late master. You had me fixed in your mind perhaps as a peasant, a lone hunter-trapper. Which of course I am now, but many years ago I made things, many things and not just cups.'

'It surprises me that I should blunder about in a snow-storm and then be rescued by a man who had himself once been a master potter, yes, sir.' Baku said.

'How long were you blundering about, as you put it?' the huntsman said, refilling Baku's cup.

'I left the river and walked through the trees. It felt like just a few hours ago. I walked on through the woods, the snow got worse, and finally it got dark, and I will admit I felt I was lost for ever, for sure.'

'There is no river, at least not one that is just hours away,' the huntsman said quietly. 'You must have been walking for at least a day or a night to have come from the river. There are little streams and there is a lake about three hours away, but the big river would take longer to walk from.'

'No, I only just left the water behind me, it was a wide rushing torrent, there was a jetty and a ferryman's hut—' he stopped then, not wishing to give too much away.

'I would say you have travelled further than you think, perhaps in a cold fever, a white delirium.' The huntsman went and fetched a rolled skin. He gestured to Baku that he should come and look at it. He partly unrolled it across the table.

It was a beautiful map, and drawn with great skill. It was painted with brush calligraphy: there were subtle touches of colour, and watercolour mist effects painted across the trees and mountains.

'This is my land—all of this forest area. This is where

I hunt and trap,' the huntsman said, unrolling more of the vellum roll. 'Here is the lake which I mentioned to you before, just here,' he indicated a ragged area of misty cobalt-blue. 'Here is where I sometimes fish, and over here,' he pointed to the bottom edge of the map, 'is the river you spoke of. Look, a ferryman is marked here, it is one of the few crossing places.'

'I can't have come that far in all this snow,' Baku said. 'How many leagues is it to the river?'

'Many,' said the huntsman, smiling and rolling up the map again. 'I think that something unusual may have happened to you. You have been guided perhaps without your knowing it. Sit yourself down again. Perhaps some more soup?'

Baku drank off a fresh bowl of soup. 'I feel I have entered another realm,' he said. 'I think I may have a demon,' and he laughed nervously.

'I don't doubt it,' the huntsman said, smiling. 'My name, by the way, is Kaito.'

'I am Baku.'

Kaito extended his leathery hand and gripped Baku's with a surprising strength. 'Welcome,' he said, 'to the very furthest edge, of the old, and still very much Hidden, Kingdom.'

For now the white maiden rested. She faded back among the whirling snowflakes and allowed her whiteness to

77

dissolve into the whiteness all around her in the fierce night. She edged back from the amber light at the window and allowed herself simply to float as she was lifted up in fragments, higher and higher up into the sky, until the next time.

CHAPTER TWELVE

An Army of Invasion

Kaito took Baku out with him the next morning. The snow had stopped falling and it lay in a soft powdery layer, which was easily traversed with the spare set of snow shoes that Kaito had supplied. Baku tried to stay warm, wrapped in the furs and skin coats that Kaito had also provided, but it was no good. He felt cold through his bones and all the way down to his soul. Baku could finally see how secret and hidden Kaito's house was. How neatly it was tucked and hidden in among the dense trees, with its turf roof and weathered door, and what a miracle it was that he had been found there at all.

They set off just after first light. Kaito wanted to show Baku the soldiers' camp. They skirted the very edge of the forest, always keeping just behind the tree line. After an hour or so of walking Kaito stopped, and crouched down, and he gestured to Baku to do the same and keep quiet. Baku distinctly heard the characteristic bit-jingling of a horse and rider. Kaito gestured to his own eyes and then Baku looked carefully around the tree trunk. A lone warrior on horseback was patrolling the edge of the forest. He wore a long cape, which hung down his back and covered the back part of the horse as well. His fish-scale armour caught the light and reflected it in sparks and flashes among the trees. He had a lance tucked behind his saddle with a small white banner flying from it. The banner was deep but narrow and had a black design of an open-fanned peacock's tail at the top. Baku could see the horse's breath steaming, he was that close. He certainly didn't want to get any closer. He pulled himself back behind the tree and as he did he cracked a twig hidden just below the snow surface. Kaito gestured for Baku to lie low, and he crouched close to the ground.

The rider turned his horse towards the trees. He had seen the old man on two occasions before and now he saw someone else, a younger man whose face seemed familiar. He turned his head away from the tree but clicked the horse on a few yards. He lifted his arm and signalled to the other riders further off. Then he called out as loudly as he could, that he would send them scuttling and his familiar would track them, the time would come and soon. In the sky a dark shape floated on the air currents, its wings outstretched, its vision sharp. It answered its master's call and circled lower. It would follow the two figures when the time came. There were elements of the Hidden Kingdom everywhere. They watched and waited for the signs, and they would set off their beacons and alert everyone and spark the uprising unless they were stopped in time, and he had a feeling about the old hermit.

Baku heard the soldier mutter something in a dialect he didn't understand. Kaito held his palm out to Baku in a stop gesture. They waited, and they could clearly hear the individual scales of the soldier's armour clinking together as the horse approached. The horse whinnied and the rider called something out loudly in a harsh voice. Baku expected to feel the point of a lance suddenly between his shoulder blades. Instead he heard the hooves suddenly move off quickly as the horse was spurred away. He poked his head out from behind the tree and saw the warrior galloping away towards a whole phalanx of mounted soldiers. There were at least a dozen of them all stretched out in a long line, and all with the black-and-white peacock banners flying from their saddle lances.

Kaito waited until the rider was far enough away and then called Baku over to him. They watched the line of cavalry gradually vanish into the whiteness.

'You see,' said Kaito, 'what we saw was just a sliver, a tiny section, a snowflake torn from the blizzard of the main force. There will be hundreds and thousands more. This is a real invasion. It had to come again at some point, and now here it is all around us.'

'Who is invading and why do you say it is happening *again?*' Baku said, looking around him fearfully as if expecting another batch of soldiers to appear at any moment.

81

'Not here and not now,' Kaito said. 'Come, we have seen enough.'

Baku heard the flapping of birds' wings; he looked up into the sky but saw nothing. They trudged off back to the hermit's house.

Above them an armoured hawk circled with its wings outstretched as it followed them back through the trees.

Baku was even more amazed that he had ever been found anywhere near the house at all, it was so artfully disguised. The roof was made of thick layers of turf and creeper. The whole thing looked as though it was just a natural part of the forest. He was convinced now that he must have been led there in his delirium by the white maiden. Why else did he think he had seen her just before Kaito rescued him and took him in?

Later Kaito and Baku sat before the fire as the cold darkness closed in around the house and the forest. Baku had been thinking of the white maiden all day, but he had not dared broach the subject with Kaito in case he was thought to be a fool, which of course he felt himself to be in any case. He summoned up his courage.

'Master Kaito,' he began, 'those soldiers we saw, who are they and where are they from?'

'Let me stop you there,' Kaito replied. 'Before we go

any further, my good friend, I am no one's master,' and he held up both his hands, palms outwards. 'Carry on,' he said.

'I am sorry,' said Baku, shivering despite the fire, 'an old habit, from addressing my own master. Is it an invasion force, is that who they are? My master, Masumi, thought so.'

'We have today seen a tiny part of the worst the world can offer. We have seen an invasion force in the pay of the unnameable. They have been sent to destroy everything. It is the worst thing that anyone could imagine. Your master was indeed right. They are a mercenary army drawn from many forces, lured only by money and false promises of power.'

'How do you know all of this?' Baku said.

'It is my job to know, in a way it has always been my job to know. I was born to it: I watch, I wait, I observe. I have done this for many years. I am a sentry, if you like, I patrol a border, a special border here between worlds, you might say.' The old hermit's eyes sparked in the fire-light. 'I have been expecting you, or someone like you, ever since I saw the first of the soldiers arrive. You have been sent. Tell me more about how your master died?'

'His death was strange.'

'Strange, how was it so?'

'We were resting on our journey and my master told me of love ...' Baku paused and then changed tack slightly. 'He confessed something personal to me, and it was very

83

unlike him. He said he was haunted by a young woman.'
Baku was only too conscious of his promise to the ice
maiden, the woman in the dream, and the icy chill went
even deeper through him, as if her fingers had grabbed
his heart where he sat, as a warning to him. Even though
the little house was snug and warm enough with the logs
blazing so nicely, Baku was still shivering with cold and
could feel little or no warmth at all.

'Well?' said Kaito.

'Oh, it was nothing really,' Baku mumbled evasively.
'He just spoke about his past, which was not his usual
way of talking, and then in the morning he was dead, of
the cold I think.'

'And that was all?'

'Yes.'

'Not so strange, then. You are sure you are telling me
everything? That really was all? Don't be afraid now.'

There was a shriek from somewhere up among the
trees, and Baku jumped.

'Don't worry, it was just a bird, an owl I expect, catching some poor prey,' Kaito said.

'Yes, of course,' Baku said, settling back in his chair.
'The strangeness was that my master spoke so personally
to me, nothing more, and then he was suddenly gone.'

'How old was your master?'

'I think he was seventy-one years.'

'He was a good age, if a little younger than myself.
Each year is a blessing to me now, every turn of every

84

season is one that I am glad to welcome. I cannot, however, see any end to this winter now that they are here,' Kaito riddled the logs and held his hands out to the flame. 'I think your demon is at work across the land,' he said.

'Do you really think I might have a demon?'

'I don't know how else to explain how I found you, or you found me. Something, someone, brought you right to my door, and you saw for yourself how well that is hidden.'

'No, I am sure it was just luck, there are no real demons,' Baku said.

'Oh, my young friend, you have much to learn. There are demons right enough, both for good and ill.'

'Have you ever seen a real demon then?' Baku asked nervously.

'During a storm in the forest once, some years ago, I saw a thunder demon. It was rolling through the trees, shaking and tearing at them. It had a fierce red mask.'

'No,' Baku said.

'Yes, and it is indeed rare to be granted such a vision,' Kaito added. 'I had lived alone in this forest then for twenty years before I saw it.'

'Weren't you terrified? I would be.'

'Of course I was.'

Baku was more scared now than he had been before. If the demon had been real, the ice demon, maiden, snow bride, whatever she was, had singled him and his master out, and had allowed herself to be seen. She had spoken to him, extracted promises from him. He was in her power. He felt colder than ever, as if somehow she had entered his soul again and claimed him for ever with the tip of an icy finger.

'Your late master died while you were on your travels?'

'Yes,' Baku said cagily, not wanting to give too much away about what had actually happened.

'Where were you going to when all this happened?'

Baku was silent for a moment. His master Masumi had said to tell no one of their summons from the Prince. He looked over at old Kaito. Here was a man who lived entirely alone and in harmony with nature. What's more, he was a man who had once been a master potter just like his old master, Masumi. What would Masumi say? What advice would he give? He would probably fetch him a short sharp flick around the ear with his practised forefinger and thumb. 'Baku,' he would say, 'you are a fool, I sometimes wonder why I took you on as my apprentice, can you not see that this man is a brother in arms, a craftsman you can trust?' It was true he would just have to trust him, he had to trust someone; he had a mission and he couldn't keep it all bottled up any longer.

'My master,' he said in a rush, 'had been summoned by a possible client, a Prince. He was taking samples of his pots, the Prince is a collector.'

'This is the Prince Osamu you speak of?'

'Yes, I believe that was the name,' Baku said, still warily.

'Of course, sadly your journey would have proved worthless. The Prince is no more. His palace is ransacked, overrun.'

'How do you know that?'

'Why, my young friend, I knew it the moment I saw the soldiers at their camp. The mercenaries are paid to destroy. He would have been their main target.' Kaito looked over at Baku and narrowed his eyes. 'How long have you been on your journey, in any case?'

'Two days and two nights until you found me.'

'Where else have you been since then?'

'I have been nowhere else but on the way to the palace and then, after my master died, to here.'

Kaito shook his head, 'I live alone here like this for a reason, of course. I know, like many others, as I am sure your master did, that one day the summons will come and a beacon, a comet will light up the sky, and me and thousands like me will come forth, summoned by the light, for the great battle. We wait hidden and ready, my friend, a Hidden Kingdom of goodness and courage waiting to protect everything. After the invasion, I fear that a sea of trouble is following close behind, and beside and within you, and I see great danger too, for you, for everything. I believe you are the key, and I wonder if you will be brave enough?'

'Is that what is meant by the Hidden . . .'

It was then that there was a heavy knock on the door and a gruff voice called out, 'Open up.'

CHAPTER THIRTEEN

Lissa and the Prince

Lissa walked ahead through the darkening trees, deeper and further on into the forest. She did not turn round to see if the Prince was following her. She knew he would be—he had no choice now. She kept her hand on the hilt of the sword she had taken from the dead brigand; she could still taste his blood. It was a fine sword, she could tell by the heft and balance. Stolen post mortem, she had no doubt, from some innocent traveller, and a high-born one at that. This was a very dangerous place, and she was the only one with any fighting knowledge, spirit or any savvy at all. The Prince was arrogant and played the innocent. He appeared to have no idea about anything except music, pots, and poetry. He had been taught all of the mythology, all of the legends—he must have known the prophecies and the possibilities of the coming cataclysm. He had turned his back on it all, and that wasn't going to get them or the world very far. And it was, after all, the very world itself that was at stake now.

She would need to find horses, or some way of moving fast through the night, or her job would be over before it had begun. If the brigand had been working alone then that was one thing. If there were others, then that immediately suggested an encampment or a hideout somewhere, and in turn that meant horses.

She stopped and closed her eyes and listened.

She could hear the Prince stumbling along behind her. 'What is it?' he called out, noticing that she had stopped. 'Tell me.'

'Ssh,' she said, 'listen.'

The Prince stopped thirty or so steps behind her. He could hear things; rustlings among the trees, the wind sighing through the upper branches, a distant owl. Lissa heard more and she smelled things too. The wind carried the smell of smoke, faint but tangible, and there was cooking meat too, and, for an instant, as the wind shifted, she caught the echo of a laugh—it was snatched away in an instant but it had been real. The Prince moved closer behind her and stamped his boots.

'I will be dead of the cold soon.'

'We will be dead of something much worse soon enough,' Lissa said. 'Now, be quiet, please.'

'You keep telling me what to do,' the Prince said angrily, 'I will not be told what to do, I am the Prince Osamu.'

'I am very well aware of who you are, Your Majesty, Your Highness. I am also aware that you are helpless, and left alone you would be as sadly doomed as one of those poor little fledglings that you will see sometimes, pink, wrinkled, and featherless, lying blind on the ground, fallen from their nest too soon, the ones it would be kinder to kill as you pass. Now, be quiet please ... *Your Majesty.*'

As the Prince turned his back on her again he clenched his cold fists, bunched his long delicate fingers as if to make a punch, but knew that he couldn't, knew that he wouldn't, and that if he did then the wretched Lissa would surely punch him back. He relaxed his fingers and looked up through the branches instead. Through the ragged scraps of cloud he could see stars, the edges and fragments of the ancient constellations. His old tutor would have had him identifying them, would have told him stories about the names, and would have woven together the mythology of the stars. He could see the one that was called Orion the Hunter, it was easily recognized in the winter sky by the bow shape and the bright star at the tip.

'We must go this way,' Lissa said, interrupting his thoughts, setting off away from him and away from the pathway.

'Why?'

She turned to him. 'Complete silence from now on unless you want us to get our throats cut.'

The Prince trudged along behind her. 'I wouldn't mind *your* throat being cut,' he muttered under his breath, stumbling through the oddly arranged hummocks and piled drifts of snow. Every so often Lissa would stop and close her eyes and listen and sniff the air like a common

91

dog. Then they would shift their direction and move on through the dark trees, a necessarily slow process. The Prince almost took pleasure from the sound of their footfalls on the snow. He distracted himself by thoughts of how he might make a poem. How he would perhaps liken the faint squeaking sound at the edge of the downward footstep of his boot against the top layer of snow to an animal cry, or an insect perhaps? He felt Lissa's hand pressing suddenly and brutally flat against his chest to stop.

She turned to him, her face fierce, and then she pulled him down hard against the frozen ground in one rough movement. She whispered in his ear.

'Just ahead, smell it: a fire, smoke, and meat.'

He breathed in hard, and the cold air caught in his nostrils, and it felt like a sharp knife cutting into him, it hurt so much, how could she smell anything at all in such fierce cold?

'I heard horses too,' she whispered. 'We need horses.'

'I hate horses, they are big towering beasts with big teeth,' the Prince whispered, his breath pluming out like smoke.

'We need a horse, horses,' Lissa said quietly. 'You *can* ride, Your Majesty?'

'Of course,' the Prince whispered back. 'I just choose not to.'

They moved forward slowly, Lissa's hand held constantly behind her, palm outwards, keeping him a pace or two behind her narrow back. She will suffer for this indignity, he thought as they neared the source of the smoke. He could see it now, drifting up white against the dark trees, he could smell it too.

Lissa made him wait behind a tree while she went on ahead. She gave him the sword.

'If anyone comes just use it as best you can,' she said.

After she had gone the Prince pushed himself up as far against the tree as he could, out of the biting wind. He weighed the sword in his hands. It was heavy but balanced and he could see that it was a well-made, older weapon. There was some elaborate chasing on the hilt and there was something else, tucked against the hand protector, a line of fur. He touched it and then he felt sick. It was a scrap of leathery human scalp and a hank of hair attached to the handle by a length of rawhide. The little thread of twisted leather string dangled its macabre trophy, no doubt one of many collected by the brigand that Lissa had killed, and no more than he deserved from the look of the disgusting thing flapping at his hand. The blade gleamed a little, picking up light from the snow drifts, and if he held it at the right angle there was some reflected light from the sky where the stars were still showing in the gaps between the cloud. He stared into the reflective blade at the mirrored pattern of stars high overhead, at their scattered sweep across the heavens. Each star was a spinning world, a cosmic ball of fire and energy, and so far away. The little pattern of stars darkened as a shadow fell across the blade. The Prince looked up. A man stood over him. He was dressed from head to foot in white skins and furs. He showed his teeth in a lopsided grin and drew a gun out from under his coat. The man gestured at the Prince's sword with the gun and the Prince put the sword down on to the snow with a trembling hand. The man had come from nowhere, his approach had been soundless. The Prince had been distracted by the craftsmanship and antique qualities of the sword and by the horrible dangling strip of scalp, and had allowed himself to be ambushed by an ugly peasant.

The man said something quietly in a language which the Prince did not recognize or understand. It sounded like a collection of clicks and half giggles, as if the man's teeth were loose and clacking together. The Prince was transfixed by the wavering black mouth of the gun barrel. He was looking for the first time in his short life into the possible absence of everything, into the black hole of his own imminent death. A dark arm slid across the man's throat and an expression of surprise crossed his face before he slumped downwards on his knees, his mouth slack, his lips trying to work and failing. Lissa stood behind him with her bloodied knife drawn.

'I said to use the sword.'

'He just appeared,' the Prince said, turning his eyes away from the sight of the still living man, gurgling and bloody, sinking gradually down into the snow.

'That makes three already that I've killed for you,' Lissa said, not bothering to hide her disgust.

'Three?' the Prince said.

'This one here, the brigand in the woods, and the man guarding these two,' Lissa said.

Two silent horses stood, heads bowed, at the edge of the Prince's peripheral vision.

'Mount up. We must go at once, it won't take them long to notice what's happened. We don't want to be anywhere near when they do.'

The brigand on the ground was still twitching and gurgling. It was too dark to see any blood and for that he was grateful. Even so, the Prince picked up the sword and then sidestepped around the body.

'Remember,' said Lissa, picking up all the weapons, 'if the horse rears lean forward.' She quickly mounted one of the horses herself and leaned into its neck, patting it and talking to it.

The Prince braced himself. He gathered the loose reins in one hand, and put his left foot in the stirrup. He held on tight and remembered to keep both his hands on the front of the horse. Then he held the cantle of the saddle with his right hand and swung himself up. This was a rough horse, a barely trained animal wild and fresh from the steppes, used to whippings, guttural shouts, crops, and spurs. The Prince remembered to squeeze hard against the flanks of the horse with his

95

thighs. The animal resisted at first, lowering its head and shaking it from side to side and whinnying quietly. Lissa leaned over and smacked its flank and the horse bolted forward suddenly through the trees. Lissa was soon following and then there came the noise of shouting from behind them, and deafeningly loud gunshots dislodging gouts of snow from the branches. A bullet ripped through a tree sending a shower of sharp splinters spinning out into the air. The Prince hung on grimly to the reins while the horse careered ahead, out of control. Lissa soon overtook him and then his horse followed hers. Another gunshot rang out but seemingly from further away. The Prince kept himself low in the saddle, going with the motion as best he could but hating the sensation. He was suddenly and violently sick in the saddle, spewing out bitter bile in a thick trail in the cold air. He felt wretched, and part of him at that moment almost wished that the bullet had caught him rather than the tree. No, better still, had caught her right in the head, the violent servant girl. He dismissed the thought as unworthy at once.

He knew of course that to wish for her death was nonsense, it was just the fear talking. He knew that without her he would almost certainly be dead. She was tough and she knew how to survive, and she had saved him, but at the same time she seemed so ruthless, and so fast, and so sure, and so unlike him in every way. It was as if she were some proud and quick-witted beast, a sleek

96

panther bent on survival, and at least he could comfort himself with the thought that she seemed equally bent on his survival too.

CHAPTER FOURTEEN

Morning in the Forest

The sunrise appeared to come at once like a sudden explosion of white light. One minute the Prince was drowsily slumped in semi-darkness almost flat across the horse's neck. The next he was wide awake in shafts of bright, dazzling sunlight. Lissa slowed her horse to a halt, and the Prince's horse, still following the lead of the other, finally stumbled to a halt too. The Prince straightened up in the saddle. He was sore and hungry, starving he would have said, but he said nothing, would say nothing to betray any kind of weakness in front of Lissa.

He looked around him. It seemed that they had emerged from the umbrella of the forest and were now a little beyond the dense tree line and out on an exposed white plain. Lissa dismounted and led her horse back to shelter under the trees. She gestured for him to do the same. He stayed just where he was, high up in the saddle as befitted a Prince. He was sick and hungry. His clothes were spattered with blood and his own vomit. His cheeks were roughened with stubble. No one had come to shave him. He was filthy and no scented bath had been prepared for him, nor perhaps ever would be prepared for him again. He looked around the field. The white snow was banked up in heaps and lumps, and lances were stuck in the ground at intervals with ragged bloodied banners bearing his colours flying from them.

'They met resistance here,' Lissa said, 'brave soldiers have died protecting the wild borderlands of your palace, and here is the sad result.'

The Prince got down. The horse immediately trotted back to where Lissa stood a little way away with the other. The Prince walked about stretching his legs and arching his back, trying to shift the weariness out of his bones. He kicked against one of the snow banks, and an arm flopped out, part-covered in armour: it was mostly cut through to the bone and leathery bits of muscle and sinewed flesh still clung to it, where the scavengers had left it. He cried out in shock and there was a sudden noise as flocks of carrion crows lifted from the trees, cawing and squawking.

A field of battle, he thought, I've never seen one before. Did all of these poor men die defending me? These terrifying and sad mounds of cut-up and mangled bodies lying dead under all the snow. Who is mourning them now? He had a clear vision in his head of a cottage door with a chair set outside in the sun and a woman sitting in the chair watching the road while a young child played. He could imagine making a poem about the widow waiting for the warrior husband and father who never came

99

back. He had to fight back a tear, his eyes stung. The reality of this field of cold devastation hit him hard. He turned from the body and walked back to where Lissa was standing between the horses under the trees.

'This is such a sad place,' he said quietly, scanning the wide field. 'I am sorry. Even so, I am hungry,' he added, 'and I must wash myself. I am altogether disgusting.'

Lissa looked at him with her unflinching gaze. 'The noble dead are never sad, Your Royal Highness, they haven't the time. In any case, the horses are our first priority, we can wait.'

'I am just not used to waiting, or starving,' he said.

'Very well, it looks like there is a nice supply of cold meat out there in the meadow, not very fresh now, perhaps even a bit stringy, but they died for you so please help yourself to as much as you want, I have a fire to build.'

'There is no need for such disrespect,' the Prince said, and turned his back on Lissa.

She left him standing by the horses with his arms wrapped around himself. 'He is such a spoiled child, and a sentimental one too,' she said under her breath, 'but what did I expect him to be?' She fetched some fallen branches, and scraps of wood and moss. Those that lay nearest to the trees were protected from the snow and so were reasonably dry. She took them to a spot clear of trees but well inside the tree line. She scooped a hole in the snow down to the ground, and flattened the sides as best she could. She built a pyramid of twigs and branches over the fragments of moss, dry wood chippings, and scraps in the hole. She went to the horse and fetched a blade. She had some tinder in her bag and she struck sparks into the centre of the pyramid. When some of the moss caught she went on her knees and blew gently, encouraging the flames. Eventually a good fire was blazing and she fed it with some more dry logs and twigs.

She went over to the Prince. 'Warm yourself,' she said. Then she moved off and out across the field.

He watched her as she rummaged about in one of the mounds of snow. He was terrified at what she was about to bring out—perhaps she was really serious about eating the dead flesh of the noble dead warriors? He wouldn't put anything past her.

She straightened up and he saw that she was holding a flat shield and a helmet. She brought them back to the fire, heaped snow into the helmet and balanced it on top of the shield over the fire.

'Water,' she said blankly, in response to his expression.

She took her bow from her shoulder and went back out into the meadow. She skirted the edge of the trees, walking with the bow raised, an arrow held tight against the string.

The Prince watched the snow melt down in the helmet, watched it gradually dissolve from the centre out. He thought of ways he might describe it in a few crisp lines of poetry, the way the snow melted it almost looked like

101

a web, that the unevenness of the flames melted different areas of the greyish snow at different times. He thought of the grey-blue glaze on one of his favourite pots and then remembered that it was smashed on the floor of his bedroom.

'I could have killed you then,' Lissa's voice came from behind him. She threw a brace of dead rabbits down near the fire. 'I could have been anyone walking up behind you.'

'Well you weren't, unfortunately you were yourself.'

'Is that supposed to be clever? I am not clever, Your Highness, so don't waste such things on me.'

She allowed the water to cool and then she watered the horses. The Prince sat himself on a log near the flames. He was close enough to feel the heat, but far enough away from the dead rabbits with their sad glazed eyes and clean white scuts.

'We can't stay here long, they will soon track us,' Lissa said, taking up one of the rabbits. She produced her knife and quickly cut the head off. The Prince looked away.

'You really should watch and learn,' she said. 'You may have to survive without me, without anyone. How will you manage?'

'You're disgusting, it's disgusting,' the Prince said, looking fixedly at the clean patch of snow at his feet.

'You are full of disgust, Your Highness. We cannot afford disgust in our position.'

She cut off the lower part of the legs.

'What is our position exactly? Do enlighten me.'

'We are far from friends. We must treat all we meet now as a potential enemy until they prove otherwise. I have the keeping of your sacred body as well as your immortal soul.'

She held the rabbit and pulled at the skin and fur, which she sloughed off with a ripping noise in one fast tug. She made a long cut down the centre of the body and pulled out the innards in a wet red rush. She started on the other rabbit.

'You will be glad of this in a minute,' she said. She chopped up the rabbits and then balanced the metal shield on log supports over the flames. She went over to a tree with extensive roots and poked about, cutting something.

The Prince watched her as she worked, picking at things and sniffing. She seemed to know so much about the earthen things and dirt things, all of the basic blood and peasant things. She was soon back and she tossed the lumps of rabbit flesh on to the hot shield and threw in some green stuff.

'Wild garlic,' she said pushing the now sizzling meat around with the point of her knife.

The Prince looked over at her, trying to avoid seeing the splattered red mess on the snow.

'What are we doing and why are we doing it?' he said.

'We have far to go, and I must take you and protect you, and in the end I must train you too.'

'Train me? For what? You do not answer me properly. Why are we doing this, why have I allowed myself to be taken away and out into the wild world with you like this? I must be mad. Why have my troops been killed, been slaughtered in their hundreds? I must go back to the palace at once.'

'There is nothing to go back to,' Lissa spread her arms out wide. 'All of that is gone, these people here are the loyal dead, and they died vainly trying to stop an army getting to your palace, Your Royal Highness,' she said and her tone managed to make his title seem like something shameful and contemptible. 'It is all gone and finished, every last part of it burnt to a cinder, every last tiny scrap, and now they will be everywhere looking for you.'

'Who exactly will be looking for me?'

'The local brigands we have just encountered are as nothing compared to the Emissary and his riders, all of them and worse; that is who.'

'So it comes back to the old story, the Emissary after all. It is such a ridiculous name.'

'The one who seeks you is known as the Emissary. He comes ahead to clear the way for . . . why am I telling you something you already know? You know all of this, you have been taught the scriptures, you have been told of the prophecy. Well, it is happening now. It *has* happened, and the end of days is upon us. He has raised his army and now they are looking for you. Luckily for you and

104

the world, you were not at home when he called, but it was close.'

The Prince looked out across the snow-covered bodies and at the line of dark trees beyond. 'Are you telling me that the Hades prophecy is really true?'

'Of course it is true. The Emissary is just the gate-keeper. Once he is through the fissure and has raised his army, the world will soon be dead and everything on it. It will not take long.'

A cold wind blew through from the trees behind them as sharp as a blade. It cut through the Prince's fur cape and he shivered and gritted his teeth.

'The wind that just crossed us will soon seem like a warm summer breeze once the Emissary has finished his work,' Lissa said.

'I refuse to believe it,' the Prince said, but quietly, with an almost defeated voice. The smell of the cooking rabbit meat had reached them and despite himself his mouth watered and he remembered just how hungry he was. He fell silent.

'Smells good,' Lissa said. 'We can eat it soon; you will need all of your strength for the coming fight whether you believe in it or not.'

She stood up and straightened. She walked over to the horses and patted their necks and talked to them, she scraped the snow from in front of them and allowed them to feed. The Prince watched her narrow back and the graceful way she walked. Like a court dancer, he

thought almost admiringly

She speared a piece of meat from the shield. She held it in the air on the point of her knife and let it cool. Then she ate it, her eyes fixed on the Prince, and never left his face as she chewed. He said nothing, just stared back at her in disbelief.

'Next one will be for you,' she said. 'I will always try everything first, just in case. And be careful, it's hot.'

She speared another piece of scorched rabbit and handed the knife over to the Prince. He blew on the meat with delicate little puffs, and then waved his hand at it in the cold air. He took a grateful bite. It tasted too good and his mouth was overcome with the taste and drooled with saliva, and fat and spittle dribbled down his chin.

'I'm as disgusting as you,' he said, gratefully licking his lips.

There was a soft growling noise behind them, followed by whimpering. Lissa quickly pulled her bow from her shoulder and tucked an arrow against the string.

'Come out,' she said harshly.

The Prince turned and looked in among the shrubs and tree trunks. There was a rustling noise and then a dog stepped out into the open. It was one of the sledge dogs.

Lissa lowered her bow. 'That's the last thing we need, one of the dogs to feed. I ought to kill it now, put it out of its misery,' she said.

'How did it get here?' the Prince said.

'Followed us through the night. And if that dog can follow us then anyone or anything can.'

CHAPTER FIFTEEN

A Pursuit

The knock came again but louder this time. Baku could hear the metal clatter of the mailed fist against the old wood. Kaito stood up. He gestured for Baku to be quiet. He pointed to the back way out of the house.

'Go,' he said, 'take your things and find a horse somehow and ride it and don't stop until the horse does. All of this is meant to be. I knew it all along. You were meant to find me. Go now at once and do not look back. Here,' he handed Baku Masumi's travel bag and then he reached up and took something down from the shelf behind him. It was a long narrow bundle of tied-up sacking cloth.

'Give this to the Prince Osamu. I know now that you are meant to find him, it has all fallen into place.' He gripped Baku's wrist and stared intently at him. 'Guard this with your life,' he said. 'Use it if you must, it will save you when it has to.'

Baku, bewildered, took the bundle. 'But . . .' he started to say.

'Go now, at once, before it is too late.'

Baku was pushed on through to the dark end of the little house. Kaito called out to the door, where the banging had started again. 'I am coming. I am slow, be patient with an old man.'

Kaito tore his way through a bundle of cloaks and outer clothes which were hung in heaps over the back entrance. He pulled a cloak free, threw it over Baku's shoulders and opened the door on to the cold darkness.

'Go,' he said, and pushed Baku out and carefully and quietly closed the door shut again.

Baku panicked. He sensed a terrible danger. He could hear the jingle of harness and the guttural shouts of more than one rider.

He walked forward; and he did not look back.

He stepped out into the snow and straight in among the close trees. He moved forward fast. He swerved off the path and then back on to it again, skirting around the tree trunks. He walked blindly on, not daring to stop and look back once. His heart was racing and his breath was smoke. He barely noticed the cold, he couldn't have felt any colder if he tried. He just concentrated on going forward as fast as he could, the cloak flapping on his shoulders, the sacking bundle clutched tight in his arms across his chest as if it were a baby.

'Find a horse,' Kaito had said. Where was he supposed to do that? He ran on among the trees, barely able to think at all, knowing that he had to get as far away from poor Kaito's house as he could and in as

109

short a time as possible. The sky above the trees was black, and, as far as he could tell, starless. The night pressed all around him from all sides. The dark trees laden down with snow, the even darker spaces between the trees where Baku knew anything might lurk— soldiers, wolves, anything.

He wondered briefly at the thing he held in his arms. It was flat and hard, it felt like a sword.

Finally, after half-running, half-walking for what seemed like hours, Baku stopped, breathless, behind a wide tree trunk. He did not dare look behind him. He tore at the sacking and revealed just what he had expected: a sword. He took it from the scabbard and it gleamed dully back at him, soaking up what little light there was among the dark trees like some thirsty traveller at an oasis. It was in very poor condition but had obviously been well made and by a craftsman. He held it by the handle and moved it once through the air. The blade rang very faintly, like a tuned temple bell, as if it were keyed up and waiting to strike, and he felt a faint ripple of energy travel up his arm.

He quickly tucked the sword back in its scabbard and put it in his belt. He had never used a sword in his life, had hardly held one before. He wondered if he would ever have the courage to use it.

He stepped out from behind the tree and carried

on, part trotting and part fast walking as best he could through the drifts of snow. It was not long before he heard the sound of a fast approaching horse from somewhere behind him. He stopped for a moment. He did not even turn round. His heart sank. He was sure now that his own death was approaching. He could hear the armour clanking and the soft thunder of the hooves getting louder. He looked away through the trees beside him. Part of him was just rational enough to think of looking for a hiding place. The dark trunks stretched away into what looked to him like infinity. The trees were an endless procession, a vanishing perspective of black verticals, broken only once . . . and not far away. There he saw an oddly familiar white shape, and thought he saw a beautiful white face looking back at him. He felt his concentration slipping.

There was a sudden loud clattering of metal and armoured horse. Baku turned and there was the warrior mounted with the peacock-tail banner on his lance. Baku's mind went blank, and he stumbled forward, thinking to outrun certain death. He blindly swerved from tree to tree, dodging this way and that, as if this might somehow fool the pursuing warrior, who simply trotted behind him, like a big cat playing with a tiny mouse.

Baku stumbled forward, unbalanced, into a clearing. There were no more trees to act as cover. He was exposed now. Something painfully sharp prodded him hard in

111

the back and he pitched forward into the snow. He rolled over and there was the fully armoured warrior on his steaming horse, standing still above him, savouring the moment before the kill. His lance was held loosely in one hand pointing down directly at Baku's stomach. With his free hand the grinning warrior drew a line across his own throat.

Baku scrambled away awkwardly, like a crab scrabbling sideways across the snow. His mind was empty now, he was aware only of his heart thudding like a drum in his narrow chest and his driving urge to move away fast. The warrior simply clicked the horse on with a jab of his spurs and followed him.

There was a sudden spiral and flurry of white, as if half the ground had suddenly risen up in a whirling wind. The horse reared up in shock, and the warrior fell heavily off the saddle and onto the ground with a thumping clank. Baku stopped scuttling. The warrior was flat on his back. The horse had run on a few paces and was breathing out heavy steam through its lowered nostrils. Baku pulled himself up and stood shakily. The warrior was spread out on the ground on his back like a turtle.

The horse was his to take.

He had no time to think about it. He panicked. Should he get on the horse and ride away as fast as it would let him?

Or . . .

He could kill the warrior first.

Then he could take the horse. Which to do?

He had hardly ever ridden a horse.

He had never killed anybody, or anything much, except perhaps mosquitoes, flies, the odd wasp.

The winded warrior was getting his breath back. He grunted and rolled onto his side. He would be up on his feet, he was grabbing at his lance and he would surely kill Baku now.

Another gust of wind, ice, and snow spiralled up between Baku and the warrior. The snow maiden, my demon, once more, Baku thought. He automatically pulled the sword out from the scabbard in his belt. It appeared to come alive. There was a flash of blinding white light from the edge of the blade. The ground rocked too, as if there had been an earthquake, and Baku rocked on his feet in turn, almost losing his balance. He held the sword out in front of him with both hands as the warrior started to stand, shielding his eyes from the blazing glare of Baku's blade. Baku, trembling, not realizing fully what he was doing, took a step forward gripping tightly the now bucking sword, not believing that he might be really about to use it. He felt like somebody else, no longer the coward Baku. The warrior was on his feet, his lance up and pointing at Baku. It would surely pin him to the ground if he did nothing.

Baku suddenly shouted at the top of his voice. It was either a scream, a grunt, or a roar, he wasn't sure which, or

113

why he was doing it. The horse took fright at the noise and stepped away back further under the trees, shaking its lowered head. Baku slashed out wildly with the dazzling sword. He too was blinded by the flickers and flashes of intense light from the blade. He moved forward, his eyes tightly shut, partly against the light and partly to distance himself from what the sword seemed to be doing as he felt the sword moving itself. Baku slashed blindly, as if simply attached to it. He held it as far away from his body as his arms would let him. He was rewarded with a sudden scream and a jerky stop as the sword struck hard at what felt like metal. There was a searing clang of metallic resistance and then he was able to complete the stroke; the resistance had suddenly vanished. The sword moved again and again very fast as he stood there with his eyes closed.

He opened his eyes.

The warrior was back on the ground staring upwards with wide but sightless eyes. Baku looked down at him as the light from the sword blade faded. He could see gouts of blood seeping out in several places between the sliced scales of the warrior's armour.

He was sliced up into neat sections.

What had he done?

'Sorry,' he said nervously to the sections of armoured body lying in the snow. 'Sorry. I am really sorry.'

He looked around, as if expecting a hand on his shoulder and a scowling magistrate to appear. There was nothing and nobody but the horse, the freshening wind and the sliced up pieces of dead warrior. He looked down fearfully at the blade in his hands. It was dripping blood on to the snow. For the first time since he had seen the snow maiden in his dream, he felt warm

He rubbed at the blade frantically with the ragged bits of sacking. He cleared the smears of blood as best he could and wrapped the sword and scabbard up again and tied them round with the string. The horse walked towards him, its head still lowered. 'Nice horsey,' Baku said nervously, as if he were a frightened child, which in some ways he felt he was. He reached his hand out and stroked the horse's head. The horse shook its mane but did not run off. Baku looked at the saddle and then at the stirrups. He tied the sacking parcel to the saddle pack and then lifted himself up into the saddle. The horse seemed to accept him. Baku made the clicking noise with his mouth that he had heard better riders do. The horse moved forward. Baku clicked again and it stopped. He got down from the saddle and picked up the lance with the banner and put them back in the holder behind the saddle. The banner fluttered in the wind. If he looked enough like a warrior from a distance he might be able to get further unchallenged. He mounted and made the clicking noise again. Horse and rider set off under the trees. Baku turned in the saddle and looked back at the sprawled pieces of the warrior. 'Sorry,' he said again out loud, and he thought he saw the woman in white spin

115

round somewhere nearby in a wind-driven flurry of snow, and rise upwards.

Baku had no idea how long he had been riding. It was suddenly morning with a pale lemon light in the sky. He had slept in the saddle and the horse had apparently trotted on through the maze of the forest unguided. The animal was tired and had slowed to an amble. Baku clicked him to a halt. He got down from the saddle and stood on the cold ground. He stretched and arched his back. The wind was strong now and it howled and crackled through the trees. Carrion crows were pecking away at what looked like a soldier's corpse half-buried in the snow. They seemed greedy for the torn flesh that showed through the gaps in the armour. Baku shuddered and clapped his hands, and the black cloud of crows rose cawing into the cold air.

He checked for the sword, his dangerous charge, wrapped in its length of drab-coloured sacking, which was now patched over with dark bloodstains. It was obviously a powerful and enchanted weapon; a sacred prize, and it was his terrifying burden too. It was still safely there strapped beside the saddle. Baku presumed it had originally been disguised in humble sacking by Kaito so that no thief would want to steal it.

Looking around at the new open landscape and the road he found himself on, Baku would have welcomed the company of anybody, even a thief. It looked a desolate and gloomy place already ravaged by the invasion, if that was what it was.

He allowed the horse to drink its fill from a puddle of snow melt. The water was the same colour as the sky, and the sky was grey like the Dobai glazes favoured by his master. Baku thought of Masumi for the first time in a while as he looked up at the low dark clouds. He thought of Masumi's body lying still, cold, and complete, under the thick blanket of snow. Perhaps, though, carrion birds like the ones he had just disturbed had already eaten all of his master's flesh by now. He wrapped Kaito's heavy cloak tight around his shoulders. The wind was building across what looked like a completely ruined and devastated land. How had all of this happened so quickly? He was exhausted and starving. He would have to find some shelter and something to eat soon. He walked on, tugging the horse after him.

Then he heard howling coming from the trees. It echoed around him as if he were surrounded. He mounted the horse and rode on. The sound of wolves grew louder. They were surely in pursuit.

He spurred the poor terrified horse on. Strange shadows flickered and moved across the roadway. He could hear the pack of wolves as they approached. Then he turned and saw them. These were not normal beasts: they were surely some sort of hound from Hades.

They soon caught up with him. He was aware of

them, scampering and thudding behind. Then he saw out of the corner of his eye that a huge wolfhound had caught up with them. Its head turned to him and its eyes were bright like flame. These were surely no ordinary earthly creatures, but something worse, creatures up from Hades. Another hound ran on the other side and it leapt up suddenly and bit into the horse with its wide open jaws. The horse screamed in terror. The creature hung on to the horse's neck. The horse shook its head from side to side. The wolf beast clung on with its jaws. The horse's front legs buckled under Baku and he fell forward, thrown from the saddle, and rolled onto the ground. The wolves were soon onto them. It was as if they had been waiting for him. An advance guard from the depths, a small part of a greater force spreading throughout the kingdom.

Baku struggled to his feet. He was surrounded. He panicked as he counted seven wolves. Each was nearly as tall as the horse. They really were the beasts of Hades. His lance was crushed somewhere under the horse. He had no weapon. Three of them watched him, circling and getting ready. The other four tore at the horse. He could hardly bear to hear the poor animal's screams. He had to do something. Everything had turned into a bad dream since he had left Kaito's hut. In a blind panic he kicked out at the hounds, then rolled back down to the ground in fear and tried to make himself as small as possible. He felt them then start to rip at his cloak. He could feel their teeth as they clashed, gripped, and tore. He had just the one weapon.

He had no choice.

If he didn't get it he would soon be as dead as the horse. If he died his promise would die with him. If he died then perhaps, for all he knew, all hope for the kingdom would be lost too—not that he should care, but the ice maiden had made him hers. She was terrifying and beautiful and he wanted to please her. The terrible warmth-giving sword lay strapped to the side of the saddle. He rolled over and over across the ground towards the horse while the wolves bit at him. He could feel the hot blood from the horse. He could see the animal's freshly exposed ribs, the bones livid white in the red darkness. The hounds' teeth were ripping through his cloak. It would not be long before they tore through to his skin, blood and bone too.

Baku lifted himself onto his elbows. The horse's back was facing him. The sword was still strapped to the upper exposed flank. He grabbed at it, and ripped it free from the bloodied sacking. All the while the beasts snarled and snapped and howled, their grey muzzles bloody. The blood dripped from their jaws and their eyes shone with the excitement of the kill. Baku stood up straight and saw a haze of white spiralling on the road before him. He saw her face clearly, and her arms as she raised them up, her hands joined, as if to say, 'Use the sword.' Two of the beasts suddenly clamped themselves to his cloak. He needed no further bidding from the ice maiden. He swung the noble weapon once, and the blade rang once more, loudly like a clanging temple bell, and as it rang it sliced the hounds' heads clean from their bodies in a great fountain of steaming black blood. The other wolves fell suddenly silent. They backed away. He held the shining bloodied sword up high above his head. He felt the renewed heat course through his own body, as if his blood had come alive again at the very moment that the hell hounds' blood was spilled across the snow. The remaining wolves stepped back further, their shoulders hunched, their heads low to the ground.

They seemed as dazed as Baku at the speed of everything. They whimpered and bared their bloodied teeth. Baku jumped among them without thought. He felt empowered by the sword and by the ice maiden. He was just as bewildered by its power as the first time he had used it. It was as if some special controlling energy had travelled from the sword all the way inside him and down his arms to his hands. He felt a surge of great certainty, of strength, even though he didn't understand it and certainly wasn't strong. He hacked at the demon beasts with the sword again and again. He sliced through them, spilling their stinking insides out across the snow, severing necks and bodies. He killed them one after the other. He killed them quickly, with the same oddly automatic dispatch, as if someone or something else was

120

controlling his hands. Baku had no skill with any sort of weapon, let alone a heavy but finely balanced blade. At the end of the attack he stood on the black bloodied snow, surrounded by the smoking remains of the seven dead beasts.

He walked back to where the horse lay dead on its side. He was cold again, frozen right through to the bone. He had no choice now but to leave the horse where it was, surrounded by the hideous remains of the slaughtered beasts, which were slowly turning to acrid smoke where they lay.

'The crows will soon clear you, poor horse, they will take you back to clean bone,' he said. He felt all power and certainty drain from him as he wiped the sword blade in the mushy snow at the side of the road. He felt like Baku again, scared and alone.

He looked around but there was no sign of her, the ice maiden. She had vanished back into the darkness. She had floated up, perhaps, and stretched herself out into the lingering icy mist that now hovered among the upper branches of the trees. At least he had felt comforted by his glimpse of her and her presence. He looked behind him, fearfully expecting something worse than the wolves to be approaching out of the darkness, but there was nothing but the icy wind and the screech of a bird of prey as it circled away over the bleak trees. He tucked the sword back into the scabbard nervously and put it through the loop in his belt.

He was alone now in the most hostile country he had ever seen.

He would have to walk through it until daylight.

CHAPTER SIXTEEN

Now They Were Three

The dog stayed with them. The Prince couldn't bring himself to do anything about it and Lissa seemed, at the most, indifferent to the animal. It just followed them that day across the cold remains of the battlefield, walking behind the Prince's horse across the covered mounds of the dead, and it stayed with them. Sometimes it trotted behind the horses and sometimes it ran on ahead. It behaved itself, and Lissa saw that it might have its uses, if only as an advance guard against danger. It seemed especially sensitive to noise and movement. More importantly, the dog responded quietly. It would suddenly stand stock still, look directly at what had disturbed it and quietly growl. It might just be a bird in a thicket, in which case Lissa would soon bring it down with a quick arrow and another meal was provided. The dog would wake at night at the slightest disturbance and still it would not bark, but simply stand upright and nuzzle Lissa awake quietly.

'Good dog,' she said to it one night, almost affectionately, when it woke her after a deer had crashed through some nearby undergrowth. Lissa set off and stalked the deer and brought it back draped across her shoulders. The Prince had woken in a panic, finding her and the dog gone.

'We were right to keep this dog,' Lissa said dumping the body of the deer on the ground.

The Prince, as ever, turned away from the sight of the dead animal. It lay with its proud antlers and its tiny feet tied round with strips of rawhide. He thought about the antlers and the image of a warrior on a horse came into his mind. He was armed with a sword and he had just such a pair of fine antlers set on his helmet. It was perhaps from a ballad or an epic poem he had read in the palace library. It troubled him, and he felt compelled by the image. He turned to Lissa, who was busily hanging the body of the deer from a branch ready to dress it.

'Keep the antlers,' he said.

She turned and looked at him. 'Having this whole carcass means we can stay here near the good water, and for the rest of the winter, possibly.'

The Prince nodded and stared at the antlers. It was a young animal and the antlers were not too large. They would fit a helmet easily. 'We must make a real shelter,' he said.

'We, Your Majesty?' Lissa asked. 'You mean, you would help?'

'We must be safe. I can see that we can't just travel all

the time. I need my palace back, my throne, my kingdom.'

'You have none of those things left, Majesty.'

'I know, but I will get them back, I see it now. The land is still there, it is all around us.'

The dog walked over to him and the Prince, without looking at it, reached down and ruffled its head.

Lissa noticed the movement of his hand, and thought, A sign of affection, of humanity, there might be some hope for him. She took her hunting knife and went to split the deer. The Prince turned away then. 'I will save the antlers for you, Majesty,' she said, before drawing the blade quickly down the pale belly.

The Prince walked away from the coming evisceration. There was only so much blood and guts he could look at or be near. He walked down towards the river and the dog followed him. He sat on a boulder, which was soft with moss and near enough to the swift water. He closed his eyes, breathed in the cold, pine-scented air and listened. The water was moving fast, snow melt had swollen it and it was gurgling and tumbling over the rocks. The Prince listened to the water. He imagined making a new poem about a river god or water demon being tickled by his own waters, so that the tumbling waters sounded with his laughter. The dog brushed up against him and he reached his hand down and ruffled its head again. He tried to concentrate on the water sound and the pattern of his poem but he was drawn back to the image of the antlers on the helmet of the mounted warrior. He imagined him on a hill at the head of an army. He couldn't shake the picture from his mind: he knew that somehow one day he would actually see that warrior. The dog lifted its paw and put it on the back of the Prince's hand. The Prince opened his eyes and looked down at the dog, which was looking up at him with big trusting eyes.

The Prince held the dog's muddy paw in his hand for a moment and he was forced to admit to himself that he was glad they had kept the dog too, and that he liked the feeling of the hot, rough pads of its foot in his hand. It felt comfortable, and comforting. He had not realized until that moment how much he needed to feel comforted.

He thought of the pots in his room, lined up across the shelf near his bed, placed so that the light in the morning would illuminate the glazes in just the right way for his meditations. He saw all his pots smashed on the floor, the boots of warriors trampling through his rooms, looting and burning. His rooms were no more. Nor were there any servants or soldiers left in the palace. It was hard to believe that his whole world had simply come to an end in one rolling blow like that.

'Who did this to me?' he said to the dog. He looked into its big, trusting, brown eyes, knowing that there would be no answer, but he asked it again anyway.

'Who?'

The dog made a kind of low grumble and let its tongue fall from its mouth.

'Who exactly is this Emissary?' He turned and looked back to where Lissa was busy with the deer. 'She won't tell me anything, she parcels it all out bit by bit. She doesn't think I can be trusted with the truth does she? A common peasant and she knows more than I do about everything.' He stood and walked back to her with the dog trotting at his heels. I suppose, he thought, it is my own fault, the price I am paying for ignoring my teachers and rejecting what seemed ridiculous.

The deer had been butchered and was hung in sections from a branch. Lissa was at the fire.

'So far it appears that no one has followed us here,' she said. 'We could stay hidden here for a while. We can build something in the trees. There is water and cover and good hunting. We can stop running for a while and wait for the signs, for they will find us. At worst we might have to winter here, but I think it will be sooner than that.'

The dog nuzzled around the Prince, pushed its big head against his hand, and the Prince once more involuntarily stroked it. 'You talk in riddles,' he said absently.

'You like the dog too, then,' Lissa said, with a half smile that the Prince could not see.

'It followed me to the water.'

127

'It likes you, Your Majesty.' Lissa said. 'Dogs are like that: they just are. They like, they love, they don't have to think about it.'

Chapter Seventeen

A Shelter

The next morning they walked along the riverside, the dog running ahead and then waiting, tongue lolling, for them to catch up. The banks of the river were dense with willow and shrubs all covered over with snow.

As the morning wore on Lissa pointed out that the snow was melting now; fat drops of water fell from the trees. They turned a bend in the river and saw a mooring jetty. It was made of stone and the sides were dark green with moss, the top mouldings covered in snow. There was even a hank of mildewed rope still attached to the mooring pole at the end. The dog went into the bushes near the jetty and vanished. It barked once. The Prince was the first to push through the shrubs behind it.

Lissa smiled to herself: His Royal Highness, the god king in waiting, really did like that dog.

A set of overgrown stone steps led up the bank away from the water. The dog was already halfway up them, the Prince chasing after the dog, pushing aside the tangle of spiky branches and shrubs. Lissa drew her hunting knife and followed close behind.

At the top of the steps there was an even denser tangle of branches. The dog pushed its way through and vanished. The Prince half-heartedly pushed at the dense mesh of sharp branches and briars. He soon gave up as the spikes and thorns dug into him. Lissa knelt down and attacked the lower parts of the bushes with her knife. She was soon able to cut her way through.

'Come on,' she called back. The Prince got down reluctantly among the slush and ice and forced his way through the short passageway that she had cut, hurting his shoulders.

'I feel like a pig,' he said. 'Wallowing in filth, as I am told they do.' He straightened up and stood on the other side of the barrier. He brushed his clothes down. Lissa and the dog both had their backs to him. Lissa said nothing, while the dog moved forward cautiously across flat ground towards a large house.

'Should we let it go like that?' said the Prince.

'Early warning. If there's a problem over there the dog will find it first. Looks abandoned to me.'

The dog reached the house and put its head down and sniffed around. A piece of dull fabric blew in and out of one of the windows on the upper floor. There was silence apart from the water and some wind high in the trees. 'Come on then,' Lissa said. She walked forward purposefully.

* * *

They went in through one of the window spaces. It had once been a fine house, built perhaps for a rich merchant. There were two large rooms on the ground level, a good carved wooden staircase, still intact, but with encroaching weeds now growing among the treads and banisters. There was a kitchen at the side with a big solid brick oven and stone canopy, and beyond that there was a bath house, with four mosaic-tiled tubs in good order, complete with their wooden lids. There was a smell of decay, even in the cold. Lissa went over to the baths. 'I wonder why the lids are still on, tight like this,' she said. 'Good place to hide a body, I suppose.'

'Oh no,' the Prince said. 'You don't think . . . ?'

'Who knows what has gone on here. Why is the place abandoned like this, and for how long, I wonder?'

She walked over to the first in the line of sunken tubs. She reached down, pulled at the wooden handle and lifted the lid. She squatted by the side of the tub.

'Nothing,' she said.

The dog was already sniffing at the next one, and scraping his paw across the wood. Lissa moved on and lifted it.

'Ugh,' she said.

The dog barked once.

She reached in and pulled out a heavy looking bundle of tightly wrapped cloth. She held it at arm's length and then threw it down on the floor. The dog approached it, sniffed at it and then stepped back.

131

'What is it?' the Prince said. 'Looks disgusting.'

'It *is* disgusting. Someone was storing their meat in here a long time ago. Looks like they left in a hurry.'

'Like us,' the Prince said.

The other two tubs were empty.

The roof was partly intact and most of the walls too. Some of the windows in the front facing away from the water were still shuttered and glazed. Where the windows were broken, plant life had already grown over and filled in the gaps, so that the house was mostly closed in and was surprisingly warm and sheltered. The walls had been mainly stripped but there was a table left in the room at the front near the staircase. There were bits of old pots and pans scattered near the kitchen.

'This would be a better hide, better than building a shelter, anyway,' Lissa said, looking round and touching the dry walls, 'we are still near the water but high, and with a good view out over the forest on that side.'

It was true, from the front upstairs rooms there was a commanding view of the approach road between the banks of trees. 'We could be safe here for a while,' Lissa said, aiming down her arm as if about to fire an arrow and looking across the tree tops.

* * *

132

By evening they had moved the horses up along the route through the trees and stabled them in an outhouse.

Lissa said, 'You can hardly see any of this house from the road, and that's just how we need it to be.'

The Prince made a space for himself at the back of the house within hearing distance of the stream. It reminded him of the sound of the fountains in the courtyard beyond his rooms at the palace.

Lissa spent some time going from room to room looking for things that had been left behind. There were drapes and rags, bolts of stuff, lengths of fabric and random bits of scattered furniture. Someone important had once lived in the house. Where had they gone, she wondered, and when did they know it was time to leave? It looked as if the house had been empty for a long time. Someone somewhere must own it.

The Prince, she noticed, had separated himself from her as soon as he could. He obviously could not wait to shut her out, to be able to close a door against her, no matter how flimsy and ruined. It didn't bother her.

The dog was in the room at the front with his paws up on the sill looking out across the landscape. She pulled him down and put him out of the room. 'Go and find him, go on,' she said. The dog stood on the landing between the two rooms looking lost. It finally went and scratched on the Prince's door. The door opened and Lissa quickly stepped back into her own room, while the dog went on into the Prince's.

The Prince sat on a dirty cushion in the middle of the empty room, his private domain for the time being. The dog came and sat next to him, and the Prince, certain at last of his solitude, flung his arms around the beast's neck and laid his head against its chest. He could hear its heart beating and the Prince closed his eyes tight trying to stop hot tears of self pity spilling out on to the poor creature's coat. He held the animal for a while, sitting pressed close in the dark room with the sound of the river demon in the running water. He did not cry but it was close. He distracted himself from his misery and hunger by trying to complete the poem in his head about the laughing river God. He would do anything to stop dwelling on the horror of his situation, the hateful cold, the ruined house and the brutal and bloody peasant Lissa. The dog at least was warm and did not look back at him all the time with a mixture of pity and contempt. He could sense Lissa's hatred of him boiling off her all the time like steam. Even when he was simply riding behind her, looking at her rigid back, it seemed to him, in his present mood, that she managed to give the impression of hate from just the set of her neck and shoulders.

He had bundled together some old curtains for bedding and he had a pack roll from the brigand's saddle which would do as his pillow. On the other nights he had crashed into a dead sleep from exhaustion. Now he lay in a cold, dark room faintly warmed by a sledge dog, but unable to sleep. He stared up at the ruined ceiling covered over with brittle, dead-looking fingers of dried-out creeper. He thought of the dressing screens in his room in the palace with their layer after layer of subtle lacquer, their gilding, and their panels decorated with delicate landscape paintings. No one at the palace had thought to paint a ruined ceiling, one that had been split apart and broken open by encroaching ivy branches, which were now as dry and dead as bones, scattered in patterns across the plaster. No one had ever opened a precious bottle in his bathroom and poured out the scent of rot and mould and decaying meat and intestinal offal into his bath water. No one had ever hung the dismembered carcass of a deer in the state corridor outside his door, either. He had been taken down to Hades itself, that much was sure, and he still had no idea why.

Lissa said almost nothing. She had dropped hints, made dark unexplained references to 'the Emissary' and left them hanging between them like the severed limbs of the poor deer. He closed his eyes and tried to empty his mind.

Lissa waited for an hour or so. She had hung the icon of the Prince on a little hook on the far wall and she closed her eyes and said a brief prayer. She was torn now between her sense of duty to protect the person of the Prince, and her mixed feelings about him. She still partly despised him as the spoiled aesthete that he

135

was, but since he had taken to petting the dog, even if absently, a genuine warmth had seeped in and she had to grudgingly admit to herself that she didn't hate him any more, and that she was genuinely fearful for him and what might happen when the battle came, as it surely would.

She had lined the weapons up ready against the wall where she intended to sleep. There was a quiver of arrows, her bow, her hunting knife, and the sword. If they had been pursued they would surely come on the forest side of the house where the horses had been. She doubted that they had been followed but she couldn't be sure. She had seen something that the Prince hadn't. On their way through the forests she had seen the telltale edges of an army, the ragged outposts of the invasion. The signs had all been there. Any brigands worth their salt would have seen them too. She wasn't taking any chances.

She crept out and went across the landing to the Prince's room. He was asleep, bundled up in the dirty old curtain cloth, and the dog was at his feet. The dog stirred and sat up and looked at her with its tongue out, eager. She stood over the Prince and looked down at his pale profile. His eyes were closed and his long dark lashes cast a shadow on his unblemished cheek. She could believe, looking at him in his innocence, that he really had no idea at all of his capabilities or of his responsibilities. He would soon find out. She took the dog by the scruff of the neck, not unkindly, and walked it back to her room and closed the door. She needed the dog's alertness while she slept.

The Prince woke into a solid wall of darkness. For a few confused seconds he thought he was back in his old rooms at the palace. He sat up and put his feet down on the floor. He felt grit and dirt underfoot, not the smooth marble or warm animal skin rug that he was expecting. He sighed then, remembering exactly where he was and who he was with. He reached out for the dog but that was gone too. He put his boots on and his quilted trousers. He stank, he was aware of it now for the first time. He thought he smelt like disgusting stale yak's milk, or the pelt of a loathsome wild animal. Lissa would have to clear out one of the covered tubs and heat some water; he needed a bath. He went out onto the landing. The house was still. He could hear the river outside but nothing else. He walked down the staircase, and out of the back door. He stood in the ragged garden that sloped down to the water and the stone jetty. He walked forward across the slush and snow. The cold air for once pleased him: it stopped him from smelling his own polecat stink.

He looked up at the stars and was taken up with them at once. He wondered at their distance from the world and the hugeness of everything, and the strange

137

fact of his standing in this spot on the earth and looking up and just being there. A few short days ago he had felt the huge weight of his history and destiny and his princely invincibility. He had been at the very pinnacle of a pyramid of loyal and loving people in the kingdom that surrounded him. Now they were all gone, it seemed, and he was a dirty little stinking speck of matter, lost in a tangle of harsh winter trees on a slushy river bank in the middle of nowhere. He couldn't make sense of it at all.

He set off back to the house and a voice said, 'Stop, I have an arrow ready to fire and pointed at your throat and I do not miss, ever.'

'It's me,' the Prince said wearily.

'Step forward and let me see you.'

The Prince walked into the tiny pool of light from a lantern that sat on the back step. He saw Lissa standing with the dog and her bow raised and an arrow held tight against the rawhide string.

'I might have fired first and asked questions later,' she said, 'then what would you have done?'

'Why would you want to kill me? Apart, that is, from hating me.'

'What I feel about you personally has nothing to do with anything,' she said. 'You could have been anyone at all: an assassin, a brigand, anyone stumbling about out here in the dark. It is my duty to protect you. I would have been failing in that duty if I hadn't challenged you.'

'I stink,' said the Prince, brushing past her and the dog, which followed him. 'I must have a bath tomorrow. Perhaps you would see to it.' He climbed the stairs.

CHAPTER EIGHTEEN

Work

It was early morning and Lissa went out, slamming the heavy door to. The cold hung around the outside of the ruined house like a curtain, a further frozen veil was draped among the trees. Tiny cloud-shaped crystals of ice drifted about the stark white branches and misted the wet evergreens into blurred grey ghost shapes.

By the time the Prince was up, driven from his bed by cold and fear and boredom, Lissa had gone on into the forest with her quiver and bow. She had left the sword drawn and at an angle across the middle of the table, holding down a bunch of ripped green leaves, a hint, he supposed, that he would have to defend himself if need be. She had also taken the dog with her, but she had at least laid a fire in the kitchen fireplace, and the Prince stood and warmed himself in front of it. He saw that she had left some vessels from around the house, copper pots and pans and a big iron cauldron and that all were full of water.

This was surely all for his bath. He lifted the black cauldron, and struggled to get it on to the hook suspended over the fire. It was heavy and the water moved inside it, making it unbalanced, so that finally he had to drop it down quickly onto the iron hook, where it swung slopping icy water and nearly putting out the fire. Then he took one of the smaller vessels of water and went through to the bath house. One of the tubs was less dirty-looking than the others, and he set to work cleaning it. It was the first time he had ever cleaned anything other than himself. The cold water hurt his hands, but after a few minutes the interior of the tub looked a little less grimy and he felt he would be able to sit in it without feeling ill.

He finally unhooked the cauldron and humped it slowly and inelegantly through to the bath house. As he waddled along he could feel the stark radiant heat from the blackened iron and the steaming water inside, and he had to hold it away from his body. He pictured himself looking absurd, balancing the slopping vessel. He could all too clearly imagine the shock and laughter if any of the palace staff had seen him doing something like this.

After he had filled the tub he realized that he had nothing to wash himself with. He was used to beautiful soaps, soft natural sponges, and precious bathing oils always being there, always replenished without thought or effort on his part. The ruined bathroom was bare of any kind of comfort, and there was still the lingering smell of the rotting meat store. He went back into the

141

warmth of the kitchen. Of course, he thought, the leaves on the table. He reached under the sword blade, picked up a handful of leaves and smelled them. It was sweet clover, he was sure of it. They would at least scent the water. He went back to the bath house, scattered the leaves into the steaming water and the sweet smell was released. He closed his eyes and breathed in. Then without thinking too much about it he stripped himself out of his dirty clothes and stood for a moment naked beside the tub. He remembered the last time he had been naked and Lissa had looked him up and down with what seemed like contempt. He could see her face now, her eyes travelling over his body. He lowered himself into the hot water. He rested his arms on the tiled top of the narrow tub and let his head fall back. His eyes closed. The water felt good. The heat seeped into his pale skin and he let out a long sigh of almost pleasure. He lay in the same position for a while, just listening to the wind outside and the creaking of the trees. He grabbed a handful of the sweet clover leaves and squashed them between his hands, which released more of their sweet smell, the only sweet smell he had noticed since he had been dragged from his bed. He looked at the leaves in his hands and saw little bubbles. They felt slippery, and as he rubbed his hands together it was as if he were soaping them. Lissa knew about such things, the things of the earth. He washed himself as best he could with the thin suds from the leaves.

He stayed in the bath and let the water gradually cool. There would come a point when he would have to get out and face the cold and dirt and shame of the foul house all around him. He had nothing to dry himself with, as far as he could see, but his own dirty clothes. He would have given anything then for a soft, warm towel and a pot of delicate green tea. He craved tea, his morning ritual: a bath, a massage with his favourite oils and unguents, and then tea taken in his rooms in calm and golden privacy; hot cleansing tea, clear green and fragrant and blended especially for him from an old and secret recipe. He could picture his tea master now, bowing solemnly as he came in at exactly the same time every morning. His head would be covered by a black skull cap, and his eyes would never look directly at the Prince. He would set the lacquer tray at the low table and go through the cleansing rituals with the tea bowls and the copper kettle. He would brush the inside of the tea bowl. The Prince could hear the whisper of the fine sable against the moon-white porcelain even now. It was the only disturbance apart from the distant songs of all the caged birds in the far aviary building. He could picture it all so clearly, a wide short brush not unlike one used for shaving. He reached up and touched his face at the thought. His skin was just slightly roughened. He rarely needed a shave. His beard was fine and slow-growing. 'A nice boy's beard,' Ayah would have said, and smiled as she soaped his cheek. Where was she now?

Dead, he supposed, along with the poor diligent tea master, whose name he had never known, never needed to know. 'Dead,' he said out loud, along with all of the anonymous but kindly servants who looked after him day to day. Perhaps even the poor man who had waited all his working life with a special key by the hidden exit from the palace. He was dead too, like some poor insect that emerged and lived for just a day in the light. There was a poem there, surely, if he could just find a key for it.

He ducked his head under the warm water and rubbed some of the leaves through his hair as best he could. He pulled his head up and saw Lissa standing beside the tub with the sword pointing directly at his throat.

'I could have killed you then so easily, all I had to do was hold your head under the water for a few minutes, and snap, you would be gone, and the whole kingdom would be gone with you.'

'I think you have made your point, don't you? I am not a warrior, I am not sleek and tensed, waiting for death every second of the day, I admit it. Stop trying to catch me out being off guard.'

'You must be careful, be wary, always on the lookout and alert to the possibility that anyone at all might mean you harm, and from any direction. You can't just sit in the tub and dream. Why do you think I left this sword on the table there?'

'You left the sweet clover as well?'

'Yes, well . . .' she hesitated. 'I left them both, and I fetched water for you when it was still dark.'

'I am grateful,' the Prince said, as regally and sincerely as he could with his head draped in scummy bubbles and wet leaves.

'I might bathe myself in your water after you. Is it still warm?'

'Well, yes it is,' the Prince said, disgusted. 'But why would you want to do that in my dirty water?'

'It's not so bad, I've bathed in worse. I have need of a little warmth.'

'How could you?' The Prince shuddered inwardly at the thought of his own foetid water. Hopefully his dirt and smell would be masked by the sweet clover leaves?

'I will get out, then. Leave now,' he said brusquely.

'Don't be shy. I will turn my back,' Lissa said. 'You can dry yourself on this.' She kicked a length of soft velvet across the floor to the base of the tub. She had found it pressed flat in a cupboard with some other scraps.

Then she turned her back and began to quickly strip out of her reindeer skins. The Prince stood in a rush of water and grabbed at the folded cloth and his bundle of clothes. He quickly pulled the cloth about himself.

He walked through to the kitchen without looking back. The fire had been banked up. The dog found him.

'Good dog,' the Prince said to it, ruffling its ears. He was tempted for a moment to look back through the doorway at Lissa. He had never seen a naked girl. He

145

had never seen anyone naked but himself. He was certainly curious. Lissa was strong, almost as tall as himself, and boyish in shape with broad shoulders and a narrow back and waist. Her eyes were for the most part blank and impersonal, surprisingly light in colour, greenish and glassy. He had found himself, if he was honest, drawn to their strange clarity more than once under the dark fringe of her lashes. The colour intrigued him, part meadow-green, and part brackish water. He stood by the fire and imagined that he had to describe Lissa's eye colour in a poem, and he tried to come up with an exact match in nature for it. The mossy rock he had sat on just a day or so ago was the closest. There was a mid-tone in the green layer, a softness imparted by the thin mosses and lichen, spread out like a short clipped beard across the surface. That would be the best comparison. He stood by the fire, and dried himself as best he could, his gaze firmly fixed on the dripping branches at the window.

CHAPTER NINETEEN

An Army

Baku crested a short hill. He stopped in his tracks, breathless and frozen, and held onto the trunk of a pine tree. The woods sloped down into scrubland and below that a wide plain stretched out. All across the plain as far as he could see were soldiers and horses. There were tents and bright banners and wooden structures, siege towers and lines of lower buildings, which he assumed were stables. He could smell cooking meat drifting up from the fields and he was hungry. He wondered at the size of the army. It was surely several armies joined together as one, from the look of it. Here was the army of invasion in full. The mercenary army. He imagined that somewhere in their ranks might be the two beautiful girls he had seen on the roadside a lifetime ago with his poor master. He supposed that there were similar forces moving across the kingdom from every side; where resistance was met it had been defeated. What would happen next? He shivered at the extreme cold inside himself, and at the thought of all the destruction that would follow in the wake of such a force.

He made his way slowly down the hill keeping in among the trees for as long as he could. There came a point when he knew he would have to step out and be exposed against the snow. He thought that he might skirt the plain, trudge his way around past the army, keeping in among the low shrubs and bushes.

It was then that a figure stepped out from behind a pine tree. He had his back turned to Baku and Baku froze on the spot, hardly daring to breathe. It was a fully armoured foot soldier. He had been relieving himself against the tree trunk. Steam still rose up from around the roots. The soldier set off down the hill without turning round. Baku decided to stay just where he was. The trees had thinned out but they would still give him some cover. He went and stood behind a wide trunk, leaned his back against it and lowered himself slowly to the cold ground.

He put both his hands on the handle of the sword at his belt, and he felt a little warmth, a little surge of energy spread across his hands and travel up his arms. There had been several times when Kaito's sword actually felt somehow alive under his hand, felt almost as if it were controlling him, or at least prompting him. It was inexplicable. He had killed an armed warrior with the sword. He had hacked his way through a pack of demon wolves. These were things he could never have imagined for himself in his worst nightmares, let alone actually carry out in life, and yet he had apparently done

148

all of those things, since he had taken on the task of delivering the sword, something he had agreed to only as death was banging at the door. Had he really agreed to it? The sword had been thrust at him in desperation. Kaito, God rest him, had been convinced that Baku was sent to him for the purpose. It was a far cry from stoking the kiln and preparing glazes for his old master. He reached in to Masumi's travel bag, which he wore under his robe, and pulled out the single pot he had taken with him after burying poor Masumi in the deep snow. The cobalt glaze shone out like a sudden bright clearing in the sky on a dull morning. He turned it in his fingers, appraising it. Could the Prince Osamu, the noble lord, really be the owner of such a mystical and terrifying sword and also, at the same time, the appreciator of subtle pottery glazes, a man who had sent for his master Masumi and his delicate pots? It seemed so unlikely.

The sky had darkened above the trees. There were rolling leaden clouds coming in on the wind just like the first morning Baku had set off carrying the bundle of pots across his shoulders. More snow coming and he had no shelter. He put the little pot away almost tenderly. The surface was momentarily cold even against his chilled skin, and he shivered. He stood, still hidden by the tree, and looked up at the sky again: sure enough snowflakes were falling already. He saw a white shape in the air. The shape gathered itself and fell with the thickening flakes down to a spot further over among the trees. He left his hiding place and went at once.

There, in among the shimmering white, he thought he could see her form flickering in and out of focus among the whirling flakes. The shape moved off quickly through the trees, as if taken by a gust of wind, and Baku followed. He put his trust into what he partly took to be an illusion brought on by hunger and cold. The illusion offered a better escape than just sitting in the cold behind a tree waiting to be found and taken by the soldiers. He trotted along behind the swirl of white and his mind went blank. Baku was no longer troubled by hunger or fear or anything else much. High above him, and high above the snow flurries and the whirling white, a silent hawk flew with its wings out straight and its sharp eyes fixed on the figure of Baku.

Everything became a blur of white; an empty sheet of parchment, a rolled sheet of dried clay: white snow, white flakes, the pure white, untouched surface of the snow in front of him, as yet unmarked by any footprint. The blank white stretched out in front of him as he skirted the side of the wooded hill above the plain. The wind howled and the snow was driven at him in horizontal gusts masking him from any of the sentries foolish enough to stay at their posts.

* * *

Baku found himself kneeling on a flat mossy stone at the edge of a river gratefully drinking cold water from his cupped hands. The snow had stopped. He had no idea how long he had been there. He straightened and stretched his back. He felt stiff and fixed as if he had been bent down kneeling at the water for a very long time. Looking around he saw some stone steps leading away from the stone pier where he had been kneeling. For one awful moment he thought he might have come full circle and be back at the jetty where the ferryman's boat was moored, near where poor Master Masumi's body was buried under the snow. There was no snow now. That jetty had been made of wood and this one was made of stone. The stones were cut in squares alternately dark and light as if a game were to be played across it. He walked over to the steps, climbed them and found himself on the edge of a scrubby wet garden. Drips of icy water were falling from the branches of the overhanging trees. He was about to walk forward when a voice called out from just in front of him.

'Stay just where you are, not another step.'

He saw a fierce looking girl of about his own age. Her hair was pulled back tightly from her head and hung over her shoulder in a dark plait. She was dressed in what looked like hunting buckskins and she had her bow raised to her shoulder. The tip of the arrow was pointed directly at him.

'What do you want?'

151

'A hot meal and a bowl of tea,' Baku said wearily.

'Are you a soldier?'

'You are not the first to ask. Do I look like a soldier?' Baku said, nodding down at his grubby robes and mud splashed legs.

'You wear a weapon,' the girl said looking at the scabbard tucked into his belt.

'I am entrusted with that, it is not mine. I must simply deliver it, and I will be glad to be rid of the thing.'

'If you are not a soldier then what are you?'

'Hungry,' Baku said. 'Thirsty. Can I put my arms down now?'

'No. What do you do? Are you a student, a labourer?'

'I am a very confused person. I am lost, I have no idea what is going on. I was brought here in driving snow and now there is no snow. Where can it have all gone? I was drinking from the river and when I looked round there was only rain and mud; no snow.'

'The snow stopped a few hours ago.'

Baku shook his head. 'I am really no danger to anyone. If you have even a little food I beg you to please share some with me, however little, whatever you can spare. I am sorry but I am driven to ask.'

'Lower your arms,' the girl said. 'Now walk forward very slowly.'

'That's the only way I can walk,' Baku said dropping his arms gratefully and stumbling slowly towards her.

The fierce girl walked backwards in front of him with

the bow still high and her arms tightly flexed. The arrow point never wavered. She was a fierce warrior girl indeed, and she seemed to Baku to be quite beautiful in a frightening sort of way. He noticed a ruined house on the other side of the remains of the garden. It was then that the young man appeared behind her.

'Who's this you've found?'

'I don't know. He looks like a beggar but he's armed.'

The young man came forward. He stood in front of Baku and looked him up and down. 'You look like you have been in the wars,' he said.

'Oh, I have, Master,' Baku said.

'Really?' the young man said, suddenly interested. 'You have seen the soldiers, the fighting?'

'No real fighting, no, sir,' said Baku. 'I have seen them grouping. I saw a hundred or so cavalry just the other day, and I just saw a big encampment across a whole plain on the other side of the hills. And I was once chased by some warriors...' he stopped, not sure how much to say about what he had done after running from Kaito's house.

'He says he's hungry,' the fierce girl said. 'He just begged for food like a dog or a common rat.'

'I think we could spare you a little something,' the young man said.

'No, we can't,' the girl said. 'Now go on your way.'

'I think we can spare him something. He looks dead,' the young man said fiercely.

He too wore crudely sewn buckskins, like the girl, but

153

he didn't sound like a hunter or a peasant at all, and he didn't look like one either.

'I have warned you,' the girl snapped back at him. 'I should end your misery now.'

'No, come,' the young man said, 'I insist.'

The girl kept her bow with the arrow tight against the string as she grudgingly let Baku pass.

'One false move,' she said.

A large husky dog stood in the ruined doorway of the house. The young man ruffled its ears as they passed. A fire was burning in a big open brick oven. Baku went at once and stood as close to it as he could. It would surely be worth an arrow between the shoulder blades to feel warm, he thought. He never seemed to be warm. He longed to feel some real warmth seeping into his bones. He held his blue-grey-looking fingers out to the flames.

'The soldiers you saw,' the girl said. 'Where was this encampment exactly?'

'I don't know,' Baku said, 'I don't even know where I am, I am hopelessly lost.'

'Why are you lost?' she added, the bow unflinching, pointing straight at him.

'It's a long story,' Baku said.

He couldn't speak while he ate, he was sure he would get in a muddle gabbling and eating at the same time. He was unsure of how much to give away. After all, he had no idea who was a friend, and who was an enemy. The girl seemed very fierce and protective of the young man. How much to say about his master dying, and about killing the pursuing warrior? He finished two strips of dried meat and finally said, 'I have been charged with the task of delivering this.'

He pulled the sword out of its scabbard to show them. At which point the lovely fierce girl leapt up like lightning and held the bow and arrow close at his throat. He felt himself making his foolish carp-fish face again, his mouth open and slack.

'It's all right,' the young man said, staying her hand and forcing her bow down to point at the ground. 'Let him speak.'

'I was just showing it to you, that is all,' Baku said, and he picked up another strip of the cured venison and started to chew on it. 'I came by this sword so suddenly and so strangely,' he said. 'I was given an impossible task. I must deliver this sword directly to . . .' and here he lowered his voice, 'Prince Osamu himself. It is his sword, apparently, and meant only for him. Now I must tell you a really strange thing. My master and I were originally on our travels to visit that very same Prince Osamu.'

Neither the girl nor the young man spoke.

There was a long silence, broken only by the crackling of the fire and the sound of Baku as he chewed his food

155

with his wet mouth slack. He looked from one to the other.

'What?' he said. 'Have I said something wrong?' His eyes widened in sudden fear.

'Who gave you the sword?' the girl said quietly, almost gently.

'It was an old man, he was called Kaito,' Baku said nervously. 'Why? Shouldn't he have?'

'Kaito,' the girl said. 'You found Kaito the hermit? No one would ever find old Kaito by chance or by looking. My mother trained with Kaito, and she trained me, and I know that he would have had to allow you to find him.'

'I found him because I was guided directly to him, I think, but I can't tell you how or by who. I was lost and delirious and I was in a terrifying blizzard of snow, and he somehow answered my cries for help.'

'What is your name?' the young man said.

'Baku.'

'Well, Baku,' he said. 'It looks like you have fulfilled the task you were set.'

'What do you mean?' Baku said.

'He means,' Lissa said, 'that he is the Prince Osamu.' She raised the bow once more, the arrow still drawn, and pushed the flat of the sharp arrowhead tight against his throat. 'Now, suppose you tell us the truth this time about how you found us and how you came to have the sword?'

156

Baku, eyes wide, gestured helplessly at the arrow.

The young man said, 'Take it away and let him speak.'

Baku explained his journey with Master Masumi as best he could and how it seemed he got lost after his master died of the cold, and then he had been found by Kaito, and then the soldiers came and Kaito gave him the old sword all wrapped up in sacking and told him to deliver it, and how the sword had already saved him from an armed warrior and seven wolfhounds from Hades. And how, by some other chance, he had found himself drinking by the river here. He did not mention the white maiden and how she had led him both times to where, apparently, he ought to be.

The Prince held up his hands, palms outwards, and Baku fell silent. 'It seems that you are blown this way and that on the winds of fate, like a shuttlecock. You say you are the apprentice to Master Masumi?'

'I am, I was, my master died of the cold as I said, and I buried him.'

'If you are who you say you are, then what happened to the pots that you were bringing to me?'

'I buried them with him, they were too heavy. I had carried them on my back for two or more days, it felt like weeks. I was alone, I was scared and wanted to move away from there as fast as I could.'

'You have no proof of what you say.'

'I do,' Baku said. 'You'll have to let me reach inside here,' he gestured to his tunic.

Lissa nodded. 'Go on, slowly.'

Baku pulled out the little cobalt-blue pot from his pouch. It was still wrapped in its fine pink tissue paper like a single precious fruit. He leaned forward and put it on the table.

It sat there untouched while Lissa stared at it.

'It won't bite,' Baku said.

'How do we know that?' Lissa spat back at him.

'Unwrap it,' the Prince said.

Lissa leaned forward and pulled at the tissue paper, which was wet, and still clung to the little vessel in patches. She held it out to the Prince.

He took the pot from her with care and sat down. He looked at it in silence for a moment. He turned it through his fingers. He looked at first one side and then the other. He held it a little way from him and squinted at it.

'That morning when you burst into my rooms, remember?' he looked at Lissa.

'Yes.'

'You burst in after your mother and you both pushed and pulled at me and one of my pots was smashed. Do you remember that?'

'Not really, I had other things to worry about.'

'This is the very identical twin of that same little pot that was smashed. Now, how is that even possible?'

'After what I have been through, I know now that anything is possible,' Baku said, and shook his head.

158

Lissa drew herself up to her full height, girded herself. The time had come to tell the Prince what he needed to know. It looked as though the second of the necessary signs had appeared.

'Your Majesty,' she began. 'I have to tell you something.'

'How can this pot have been brought here to me so randomly, and by this means?' he gestured to Baku, who sat munching hungrily on another dried strip of venison meat.

Lissa said, 'I don't know, but that is exactly how things happen in the Hidden Kingdom.'

Baku took notice. 'The Hidden Kingdom. That is what Kaito mentioned to me. He said I was there on the far borders of it or something, and Master Masumi too. What does it mean?'

The Prince put the pot down on the table. He arranged it carefully among the damp scraps of tissue. 'Masumi was a true master,' he said and nodded his head.

Lissa lowered the bow and spoke again. 'We live in this place,' she gestured with her arms, 'and I don't mean this old house, I mean our world. A world of seasons and beauty, of day and night, of forests and mountains and oceans. This world touches on other worlds, and one of those others is the world we know here as Hades, the place of evil and demons and the damned.'

'Are you reciting my old scripture lessons back at me?' Osamu asked.

Baku felt suddenly uncomfortable. He shivered more

159

than usual and felt himself breaking out into a cold sweat.

Lissa continued without responding to the Prince. 'Our world comes at times very close, too close, to the world of Hades. There are hidden portals, deep caves, the insides of fiery mountains, some of the frozen places where demons sometimes break through.'

The Prince interrupted her. 'You are really sounding like old Shen Zu. Did he teach you all of this old stuff as well? I thought you were just a simple, uneducated peasant girl.'

'You know nothing about me, Sire, you have asked me nothing since I rescued you, and nor do you really know anything about yourself.'

'Perhaps you would like to tell me about myself, then.'

'That is just what I am trying to do, if you will let me, Your Highness. It is written that once every seven hundred years the seven ruling demons from Hades attempt to enter this world and rule it too. If they succeed our world will be in darkness for eternity. They will make a new Hades here on earth.'

'Yes, that much I know, that much we all know,' Osamu said in a bored voice, rolling his eyes up and shaking his head. He turned to Baku, who was listening intently to Lissa. 'You see the way I am spoken to? All respect for my status has gone, my proper position is forgotten as if I too were a base peasant, unaware of the old scriptures and the prophecies.'

'I didn't know any of it,' Baku said, rising fear taking hold of him.

'You have not had the benefit of an elderly and fussy personal scholar to tutor you in these arcane things. Why, I doubt if you can even read?'

'I can read,' Baku said. 'Master Masumi taught me my letters and numbers, he said I would need them for the trade.'

'With respect, *Sire*,' Lissa said, her eyes blazing now with suppressed anger. 'No one has forgotten your position. My life is dedicated to your position, and has been since the day I was born. So have many, many others and they have lost their lives for you, my poor mother for one, and it looks like Kaito has too. He was a great man and a warrior who was hidden in the forest all these years, waiting with the sword for the sign.'

'Was I the sign?' said Baku.

'You were an unwitting sign. I saw the real sign in the sky and have been waiting ever since. Kaito knew that one day you would come in the wake of the army.'

'He showed me the army,' Baku said.

'He knew what it meant.'

'Would you mind telling *me* what it meant?' the Prince asked, sitting on the edge of the table and picking at one of the dried meat strips.

Lissa took a breath and started again. 'It means, *Majesty*, that one of the war demon's minions has breached the gates of Hades, and has come into our

161

realm. It has been busy too. It has set off conflicts within the kingdoms and has invaded this one, all of it just to find *you*.'

'Do you know what you sound like?' the Prince said.

Lissa carried on ignoring the Prince. 'These minions that break through from time to time are usually caught by sentries of the Hidden Kingdom, men like poor Kaito or even women like me. Sometimes, though, they succeed and start to carry out the wishes of their seven masters. This is what has just happened, the soldiers attacking the palace, all of that was to remove you, kill you, to get rid of you and your line for ever. The Emissary or his outriders search for you now and you must be ready, must be *made* ready to defeat him as only you can.'

'You are obviously mad,' the Prince said. 'Listen to yourself. My palace is sacked by some upstart warlord or other. A young peasant stumbles across us in our hiding hovel in exile and he carries with him a rusty old sword and a pot made by a craftsman I admire. Now, this is an odd coincidence, I will admit. But according to your mad logic two and two make five, and it is suddenly proof of doomsday and the end of the world is nigh.'

'It is, Your Majesty,' Lissa said quietly. 'I have never been more serious. Test my story, test the truth. Why don't you simply pick up the rusty old sword?'

'If I do will you stop all this stuff and nonsense?'

'If you were to hold the sword just once I won't have to stop anything.'

The Prince nodded politely at Baku, and said wearily, 'May I then hold the sword, please?'

CHAPTER TWENTY

A Rider Returns

The Bodyguard sat tall in the saddle. He gazed across the flat plain at the assembled armies. Soon they would spread out across the known world, and perhaps even beyond, subduing, enforcing, enabling the seven to emerge and rule in their rightful place. He watched a spiral cloud of dust kicked up by a fast-approaching horse and rider. He sat beneath the elaborate banner of the combined forces next to the canopy of the Emissary himself. He hoped that this might be one of the three riders returning. So far the riders had been gone for days. He had assumed that they had met with little or no opposition. The three riders had been sent across borders, requisitioned farmland and farms, organized supply lines and had kept the armies well-fed so far. He could see the reassuring peacock-tail back banner now flying bright in the spring sunshine.

The Bodyguard turned in his saddle. He wasn't sure he would ever get used to the sight of the Emissary, who was enclosed in the shade of the canopy erected in the saddle. Black fish-scale armour, a solid black helm, and a black cloak were normal enough, except that the Emissary's black armour seemed not just black, but to drain light from everything around it. It seemed somehow to suck in all the energy from the space round about him. It was hard to look at him, even though there was nothing of him to see but a kind of hidden, silent, and terrifying negative shadow.

The Emissary had despatched the three most trusted riders to follow any leads after the initial sack of the Prince's palace. It seemed to him now to have been a very long while since they had piled all those broken and dismembered bodies in the courtyard and burned them, using arrow accelerant and the contents of the wine cellars as fuel.

There was still no real and certain evidence to show that the Prince Osamu had survived the attack, or that he had died.

The horse and rider approached, and were slowed to a halt by the honour guards. The rider dismounted carefully. It was the Hawk-Master. He went down on one knee, not even daring to look directly at the gap in the tent flap where the Emissary might be seen. The Bodyguard dismounted and ushered the dust-covered rider into the campaign tent behind them with a wave of his mailed hand. He quickly poured out some wine and handed it to him.

'Well?'

The Hawk-Master gulped down the wine, wiped the back of his hand across his mouth, and helped himself to more. 'I have things to report. They might seem like nothing, just bits and pieces, but they all add up. Right after the initial attack on the palace you will remember that I took a search-and-recruiting patrol out into the territories. I stopped at an inn at the first snowfall, and among the people staying there I interviewed an elderly potter and his apprentice, who claimed that they were on their way to sell samples of his craft at fairs and markets. I looked at his wares, all very artistic stuff, just the sort of thing Osamu collected. His abandoned rooms at the palace had been full of it. I thought for a moment that these two might be travelling at the Prince's direct invitation or perhaps the palace's. I let them go, he was old and the boy seemed a fool. I now think that I was the fool. I am sure the old potter was a sleeper, a sentry. If nothing else it shows that the Prince must have been at the palace at the time of the attack at least. Later I took an elite squad of cavalry, as you know, and we went looking for any signs of sleeper sentries. One morning we saw a glimpse of what might have been a huntsman and a younger man in the forest near our encampment. We sent out my seeker. She looked for them and eventually found them. He was an old hermit living a completely hidden life. From what we found later in his hide he had obvious connections to the palace and the Prince. He

166

was a sleeper, all right, one of the old Hidden Kingdom warriors in waiting.'

The Hawk-Master drank off some more of the wine. 'He kept his old mouth shut tight until the end, too, a loyal and brave old bastard. Here's the real point: he had someone with him in his hideaway, the younger one that we saw earlier, and he got away on foot into the forest. I sent a good man after him on horseback. He never came back.

'We found him the next day. He had been cut into neatly sliced shreds and there was no sign of his horse. Then a report came in that some of his Excellency the Emissary's familiars had been destroyed by some lone rider. Spirit wolves, all seven of them in one hit I believe. The point is, sir, that the body of my man who was destroyed in the forest bore certain marks. He was cut with no ordinary weapon, and how anyone could face down and kill seven spirit wolves without having a very special weapon I don't know.'

'You think this was the Prince, then, and he was already united with the sword?'

'This showed more than training and skill. I think the old man had the sword and had somehow already passed it on.'

The Bodyguard punched his own palm. 'We can only hope that is not true. It will be the helmet next. If he has that too then he will be able to raise his own army. The Emissary has waited too long to fail now, we cannot fail.'

167

'The armies are gathered, sir, we are well prepared. However, I fear the white maiden is involved too, one of the men thought he had seen her.'

'She was seen and the man lived to tell you? Nonsense! Either she must be slipping or your man was dreaming. We must redouble our efforts to find the Prince.'

'I have my hawk out following the trail of the young guest of the hermit and she has not failed us so far.'

The Hawk-Master stepped outside into the cold air. Soon she would be back and she would lead them to the Prince, he was sure of it.

CHAPTER TWENTY-ONE

The Sword

Baku hefted the sword by the handle. 'It's not mine, so please take it. It frightens me,' he said, conscious again of that strange little flicker of energy he felt whenever he touched the sword. He felt it now but it was softening, draining away even as he held it, until the sword itself seemed suddenly rested and still. It felt at once like any other heavy piece of dull, rusted metal. 'It's an old thing but it was well-made, as you can see, and obviously by a craftsman,' he said. 'It's rusty, though, and it could do with some cleaning and refurbishing if you look, but it . . .' He stopped, as the Prince simply took the sword from him.

The room was filled with a sudden brief and dazzling whiteness. Great flashes and ripples of light played around the handle and hilt and shot up and down the blade and out in every direction around the room. The battered and dirty sword was suddenly shaking, and flakes of rust and green verdigris showered down onto the floor. The apparently rippling surface of the sword gleamed impossibly bright so that Baku had to narrow his eyes and turn his head away. The dog howled and bolted out of the room. Lissa stared at the shining sword directly, without blinking once. She smiled and went down on one knee and lowered her head.

Osamu felt a compelling certainty as he held the sword. Baku had been fearful of the unleashed energy and power. Osamu felt only a sudden sense of completion, of rightness. The sword was his, there could be no doubt. He did his best to control the flickering energized sword, but it was like holding a living thing, a wilful creature, and he had little enough strength in his upper arms. The poet part of Prince Osamu even managed to find an analogy. To that part of him the blade surface looked like the flash of rainbow seen on the scales of quickly darting silver fish glimpsed in clear water in summer. There was another part to the Prince, a darker and, so far, an entirely hidden one. It was as if picking up the sword had unlocked that other part of him in an instant. There was a surge of mysterious strength and an odd feeling of certainty, of rightness. It was as if he had always been waiting to pick up this very object, and it came over him in a rush.

Eventually, after a brief struggle with balance, he was able to lay the sword down onto the table. It chimed as it touched the surface with the clear ringing tone of a temple bell. Baku looked from Lissa to the Prince: neither said anything.

The Prince studied the sword, as it lay rippling with flashes of green light and energy. He looked astonished.

'It felt so right in my hand, alive and impossible, but as if it should be there, had somehow returned to me, as if I had lost it once a long time ago. It fitted like it belonged,' he said quietly to himself.

'That's because it does belong, Your Majesty,' Lissa said. 'It's *the* sword, the one forged for you.'

'It's a frightening thing. It made me do things I could never have imagined doing. It is a powerful weapon,' Baku said quietly. 'It saved me, just like I told you, it's true.'

Lissa moved now to stand directly in front of the Prince. She bowed her head again, her arms were held rigidly at her side, the dazzling light from the sword highlighting her dark plait and the nape of her neck.

'Your Majesty,' she said.

'What is it?' the Prince said quietly, still gazing down at the silvery blade.

Lissa stayed as she was, head lowered, Baku shuffled awkwardly to his feet and joined her in lowering his head too, so that they stood like two supplicants. The Prince reached out and gently touched the sword.

'You meant all of those terrible, mad old things that you were saying just now, didn't you? All of those old scriptural prophecies that Shen Zu tried to drum into me, all of that mythology and history I learned, everything about the demons from Hades, the evil, the demons, Hades taking over our world for eternity, every last single word of it?'

171

'It's all true, Your Majesty, all of it,' Lissa said, without raising her head. 'As I said before, the time has come.'

'The terrible thing is, I believe you,' the Prince said.

Baku stayed just where he was. He had seen too much recently to risk anything else.

'We should celebrate the safe return of the sword,' Lissa said, with her head still bowed. 'It is a solemn and important moment that we should honour with cere-mony, but sadly we have nothing to celebrate with but cold water and dried meat.'

'There is something,' Baku said. 'In the pot. You will see that it is sealed, it has wine in it.'

The Prince reached forward and picked up the little pot.

'There is a cork plug in the neck,' Baku said.

'So I see,' the Prince said. He pulled out the fragment of cork and sniffed at the contents suspiciously.

'It smells very rough,' he said.

'Good,' Lissa said, looking at him defiantly. 'We need that, we must become rough.'

'It came from a simple ferryman's hut,' Baku said, seeing at once in his mind the cold body of his master and the beautiful face of the ice maiden. He said nothing further.

The Prince put the neck of the pot up to his lips.

'No, Your Highness, it must be me first,' Lissa said.

He handed her the pot without a word. The dog came in warily and rubbed its head against the Prince, who fondled its ears.

Lissa drank from the pot. She closed her eyes and kept her mouth pressed tight against the lip and waited. The light from the sword flickered over the walls like the reflections from a sunlit river. After a minute she passed the little pot back to the Prince. He looked at the broad wet mark on the grey lip of the pot where Lissa's mouth had been. He looked down at it at first with a flicker of his old distaste and he considered wiping it clean and dry. He looked up at Lissa, her clear eyes, eyes the colour of the mossy rock in the river, that watched him from under her dark lashes. Their eyes locked and held and neither would look away.

The Prince pressed his own mouth at once to the wet marked lip of the pot and drank down a draught of the wine, still looking into Lissa's eyes. The sweetness of the wine, the first he had tasted in weeks, opened suddenly in his mouth, like a paper flower in water. 'Oh,' he said, 'sweetness I had forgotten.'

He passed the pot to Baku. 'Thank you,' he said. 'Take it, it's your turn now. Finish it, it's yours anyway.'

Baku gulped down the last of the sweet wine.

The Prince kept his gaze on Lissa, and in that instant it was as if he was looking at her for the first time. His usual day-to-day annoyance, his irritation at the sight of her, his feelings of anger with himself for his total dependency on her, seemed to have dissolved in those few short moments since he had picked up the sword. He had caught her eye while he drank the wine, while

173

his mouth was touching the wet pottery where her mouth had made its own wet mark. He had looked at her frankly, openly for once, and she had looked back at him in the same way, and it was as if a barrier had suddenly been removed between them. It was something so obvious that he had never even thought of noticing it. He could not explain it. His poetic side was suddenly fired up and busy again. Likening her eyes to moss on a river rock was not enough. He could now rhapsodize internally about every single part of her: her narrow back, the tilt of her neck, the thick plait of her hair and the way it swung heavily when she rode, bouncing against the tender exposed nape of her neck.

What was happening to him? He could only imagine the snorts of derision, the guffaws of laughter that would follow if he were to say a single word of what he was feeling now out loud. And yet he had caught her expression when she looked back at him and, in some deep part of himself, he had read and recognized that signal, that return of passionate fire as fast and sure as one of her arrows. He could not for one moment allow himself to believe it consciously, but deep down he knew it.

Outside there came the sudden shrill cry of a bird of prey, a keening screech which sent a shiver through Osamu. The dog barked, and Baku said, 'That bird must be following me. I heard that same shriek while I was travelling.'

'Following you?' Lissa said, and she rushed over to the

door and wrenched it open. She stepped outside into the weak sunshine and a bird rose up from the scrubby grass. It was either a large falcon or a hawk, she couldn't tell against the light. It circled once more over the house and made another shriek. She knew exactly what she had to do. She went back in and grabbed her bow and quiver and slung them over her shoulder.

'What is it?' the Prince said.

'I have to go, and now, before it's too late. It *was* following you,' she said to Baku.

'Wait,' Osamu said. 'I'll come with you.'

'You will stay here with him,' she said. 'I will be back soon, you will only slow me down.'

CHAPTER TWENTY-TWO

A Pursuit

Lissa was soon out skirting the forest road and pushing the horse as fast as it would go. She could see the distinctive silhouette of the bird circling high above the trees.

She pressed her thighs tight against the horse's flank and let go of the reins. She reached round and unhooked her bow and fixed an arrow to the tight rawhide. She waited, aiming a little ahead of the bird. Her concentration was all in the sky. Lissa fired her arrow. It pierced the bird, killing it instantly. It appeared to dissolve into a shower of black dust and smoke as it fell to the ground.

Ahead, around a curve in the route, a quartet of warriors was spread out. The Hawk-Master was in front making encouraging hawk calls and holding his armoured arm out ready for the bird's return. He saw the sudden arrow flight and watched as it pierced his creature, his familiar. The Hawk-Master cried out as if he himself had been struck. He spurred his horse forward pointing down the road with his drawn sword and screaming at the top of his voice.

Lissa took hold of the reins again and was about to turn and head back through the forest to the house when she heard loud cries and the thunder of hooves ahead. Then almost at once they were there on the road directly ahead of her, the armoured warriors with lance banners, and all heading straight towards her. She knew what she must do: lead them a long way in the wrong direction and then lose them before going back.

The Hawk-Master called out, 'Fire!' to one of the riders. The rider raised his double crossbow, ready-loaded with two bolts.

Lissa turned the horse and headed in among the trees. The rider fired and the twin bolts whistled past, narrowly missing her horse's flank.

The Hawk-Master's plan was in a dire muddle now. His seeker was dead, his path to the Prince closed off. He must now take the girl at all costs and make her tell them where the Prince was. They had their ways, not the least of which was the presence of the Emissary himself; a small exposure to him and most people were gibbering wrecks within a minute. The girl would talk, he was sure of it.

'I want her alive,' he called out.

Lissa made herself as small as she could in the saddle, crouching low with her head close to the horse's neck. She held on with one hand and reached into her tunic. She pulled out the pistol she had looted from the dead brigand—it was still primed and ready. She turned in the saddle and aimed it at one of the approaching riders. She fired the gun and it went off in a shower of bright sparks and with a deafening bang. Her horse bolted faster at the noise and a great flock of shrieking birds rose up from the trees.

She turned again to see that the rider had fallen. Two more crossbow bolts flew past her and slammed into a tree trunk. Great sharp splinters of wood spun out into the air and one of them tore into the horse's side. It whinnied and reared up, throwing Lissa off and onto the ground.

She rolled as fast as she could in among the trees, then got to her feet and ran to where the trees were at their thickest and the roots the most tangled. She needed to put some distance between herself and the riders and go where the horses would find it most difficult to follow. There was a dip down into a hollow area and Lissa let herself fall all the way down the slope on her backside. She could already hear the cries of the pursuing riders who would now be fanning out to find her. She needed a vantage point where she could use her bow. That hawk had been just what she feared it was: a spy for the Emissary. It had followed Baku on his wild journey, and would have led the riders to the Prince. Not any more.

She kept low to the ground and ran across the centre of the hollow. There has to be a hiding place—a rock, a cave, a hollow tree, anything at all, she thought.

Climbing out of the dip there was a series of wet rocks, long horizontal slabs like tables jutting into each other and rising up the far side. A huge fallen tree lay across the top slab. If I can just reach it I might pick them off, she thought.

Lissa scrambled up the edges and then along the flat surfaces of the first two slabs. She was clinging on to the edge of the third step when she heard loud shouts. They had found her. She doubled her speed and kept as low as possible. Making herself into a small fast target was, she was sure, the only way to survive at all. Two more crossbow bolts screamed over her head and smashed into the rock. She hadn't much time to reach the fallen tree, which would at least give her some cover. She had to risk climbing up the last rock shelf, which jutted out further than the others and was at least thirty feet from the ground. It would mean hanging exposed while she climbed.

She could hear the horses and the clanking armour as they fanned out below her. If she didn't act soon she would be trapped. She ran, crouched forward, and leaped at the overhanging edge of the shelf. She gripped the wet rock with both hands and swung herself out over the gap. A longbow arrow sliced the air a few inches from her neck and skittered harmlessly off the rock. She swung herself backwards and forwards, keeping herself moving as she pulled herself up to the flat rock, using all the strength in her arms. Two crossbow bolts flew past

179

her, splitting the wet air like angry hornets. She took one last heave and raised herself up, swinging one leg to the side.

A longbow arrow slammed into her leg. She heard the screaming whistle of its flight and ducked her dark head before she felt the stab of pain. She kept her balance, looked down quickly and saw the arrow in her thigh and her bright blood staining the buckskin. It was not deep and she could deal with it later. She swung herself onto the flat wet surface and the arrow broke as she shuffled low across the wet rock. A searing pain shot through her leg and she closed her eyes and clamped her teeth together. She would not cry out.

A vision of the Prince's face was somehow fixed behind her eyelids now it seemed. As his image swam up through the pain and his eyes locked tight on hers, she lay flat to the rock aware of the throb of agony in her leg. She looked back at the Prince inside her head and took strength from that look.

She opened her eyes and looked down into the dell among the trees: there were three riders at the bottom of the dip and one, the Hawk-Master, at the top of the rise opposite, his face obscured by armour. It would be hard for the mounted riders to hit her now as she was on the flat shelf of rock, but she might have a chance to pick them off. She unhooked her bow and lay the quiver down on the rock beside her. She tucked an arrow against the tight rawhide string and aimed the

180

bow flat along the rock, which tilted down slightly. The nearest rider was trying to make out her position. The obvious thing would have been to have made for the fallen tree, and so she hadn't. She took careful aim. There were vulnerable spots, chinks in the armour, especially under the edges of the helmet. She fired an arrow, one of the steel-tipped ones that she had looted from the brigand in the forest. It struck the nearest rider exactly where she had wanted it to—straight through his throat—and his head fell back in an arc of bright blood spray as he clattered from his horse. The horse was spooked. It reared and bolted towards the shelves of rock. Shouts went up from the other two riders and a pair of crossbow bolts slammed into the edge of the shelf where she was lying, sending sharp splinters and fragments of rock spinning up into the air.

The Hawk-Master on the rise called out something that echoed around the dell and among the trees. It was in a dialect she had never heard before, and didn't understand, but he was obviously furiously directing the remaining two riders. She slid further back from the edge of the rock and looked down at her thigh. A stub of arrow shaft remained. The head was not as deep as she first feared, and it was a military arrow, so with any luck the metal head would at least be clean. She edged forward, aware of her need to stem the blood flow from her leg before she passed out on the rock.

The other two riders had dismounted and were skirting

the dell in opposite directions, a pincer attack. One of them was fumbling with something on the ground while the other moved slowly behind the tree line for cover. Lissa quickly dispatched the one at the tree line with a well-aimed arrow.

The Hawk-Master shouted again. The fumbler managed to make a bright spark in the grey air and quickly raised his bow with a flaming arrow attached. He was aiming high, obviously hoping to hit the fallen tree and smoke her out. Lissa fired at him twice very quickly and one of her arrows pierced through his firing arm. He fell backwards and the arrow seemed to set him on fire at once. He must have been issued with a volatile liquid for just such a purpose, and the burning arrow had caused the liquid he carried to explode in flame all over him. She could not watch him burn, or hear his screams, even if he was an agent of Hades, so she dispatched him quickly with another arrow.

It would take the Hawk-Master a few moments to get with in range of her. Lissa slid back from the edge of the rock, gritted her teeth and attempted to pull the arrow head out of her leg. She would not scream. She could not pull it free. She tore off one sleeve of her buckskin tunic and twisted it tight, then tied it around her narrow thigh as hard as she could, until it hurt worse than the actual wound.

Lissa crawled back up to the edge of the rock and looked out over the dell. The Hawk-Master was busy spilling gouts of the volatile liquid and encouraging the flames among the trees. She would soon be surrounded by burning scrub and trees. She heard a horse whinnying in terror below her. The fire was taking hold quickly.

Lissa had just one arrow left in her quiver. She closed her eyes and prayed for a miracle. The sound of the fire was loud now she could hear timber as it cracked in the flames. She heard branches snapping, and trees falling. It would not be long before she was forced to move.

She looked over the edge: the Hawk-Master was walking up the other side of the dell back to where his own horse was panicking and straining on the rope that tethered it. He was setting fire to everything behind him as he walked, confident that Lissa would have to at least try and escape the flames, his only chance now to get her.

Lissa watched him, sure that he would soon be too far away and out of range of her longbow, and she was feeling weak now with the pain and the blood loss. The flames were climbing higher and roaring and she would soon choke on the dense drifting smoke. Birds were flying up cawing and shrieking from the far trees, and she could hear the thudding rush of hidden animals as they ran.

Suddenly, out of the dense smoking undergrowth at the base of the rocks, something hugely tall lumbered out. It was a black bear. Its fur was burning and it was roaring and showing its sharp teeth. It lurched forward, dropped to the ground and ran howling up the slope straight through the flames directly at the Hawk-Master. It was as if the bear had gone unerringly straight for the source of its own terrible agony. Lissa watched the Hawk-Master as he dropped the burning brand at his own feet in terror and raced away from the raging bear backwards up the slope.

Lissa rolled to the very edge of the rock shelf. The military horse, the one that had bolted after she had shot the first rider, was trapped below her between the rocks and the spreading flames. She fell onto the next level down, and then down again, bruising herself and crying out in pain, certain that the Hawk-Master was too busy escaping from the ferocious burning bear to hear or notice her. She limped in agony over to the horse. It was rearing up on its hind legs, its eyes wide in terror. She grabbed the reins, good strong army-issue reins, and then limped backwards, pulling as hard as she could. The horse came forwards with her, its nostrils flaring. She coaxed it out from the tight space it had wedged itself into. It was terrified and foam flecked its open mouth. She gently stroked it, pressed her hand flat to its head, whispered to it and then swung herself up into the saddle, almost fainting from the pain in her leg. She urged the horse on, away from the flames. The horse climbed the side of the dell and Lissa gripped

184

tight as it cantered away across the flat ground through the forest, which was now burning and wreathed in dense acrid smoke.

CHAPTER TWENTY-THREE

A Journey

Lissa emerged from the veil of heavy drifting smoke and onto the road beyond the trees. She slowed the horse, leaned forward and patted its neck, and pulled it to a halt. Her thigh throbbed in pain. It took all her strength to stay upright in the saddle. She allowed the horse to stand while she scanned the road in both directions. There was no sign of the remaining rider—either he had escaped or perished with the bear and everything else in the fire.

The flames were visible now among the trees at the very edge, and they were spreading. The wind was in the worst possible direction. The fire would not take long to reach the house and the Prince. She could not wait any longer. She turned the horse in the direction of the river and urged it on, away from the flames and smoke. As they rode she was only too aware of the fire snapping at her heels. She wondered through her agony exactly what the liquid was that could cause such fast destruction once lit? 'Something from Hades itself, of course,' she said out loud, and she could hardly hear herself above the fierce crackle of the burning trees.

Left alone with Baku the Prince had little idea of how to speak to him or engage him as an equal. He had hardly met any people of his own age before. His tutors were all older. He had no siblings, no parents that he remembered. He was someone who had grown up used to deference and protection. His conversations had been mainly with his tutors, poets and scholars, and he had developed the aesthetic and scientific side of his life to the exclusion of everything else. He couldn't kill, fight, cook or clean, or do anything much that was useful or practical. And of course he had upset all of his loyal and long-suffering tutors by rejecting their teachings on the Hades invasion. To him it was a myth, nothing more, and so he had refused from an early age to study fighting and the arts of war.

'How did your master, Masumi, die?' the Prince asked Baku.

'It was cold, very cold. He perished from the cold is all I can say. I have been cold ever since. I cannot get warm. I shall never be warm again.' Baku sat huddled in on himself. The sword lay on the table between them. It was glowing but cold, light without heat.

'When I held that sword,' Baku said, looking at it fearfully, 'it took me over, it guided me. I cannot fight,

187

I have never fought anything but the cold,' he shivered. 'It sliced an armoured warrior into chunks of flesh as neatly and cleanly as if he had been quartered by a skilled butcher. Then it took out seven wolfhounds, demons, I turned them into puddles of filthy slime and smoke using just that sword. I don't remember doing it—I didn't know what I was doing. It terrifies me, to be honest.' Baku reached out his pale cold hand and touched the handle. He felt nothing, no shiver of energy, there was no life left in it for him.

'The sword has found you,' he said. 'It felt alive in my hand once, but not now. Mine was the wrong hand, the wrong arm. I wasn't the one it wanted, I was just there to help it find the right one—you. It guided me to you and it used me. This is not a bad thing, it saved me too, but I think it only allowed me to use it because I was bringing it to you.'

'I would never have believed a single solitary moment of this just a few short weeks ago, but I am forced to now,' the Prince said. He reached forward across the table and touched the handle of the sword. The blade crackled and glowed even brighter. 'I can feel it, feel the energy, the life in the metal. Impossible, but there it is under my hand now.'

'It comes from somewhere else,' Baku said, 'that sword is either from Hades or Elysium, I'm not sure which.'

'We must hope it was forged in Elysium,' the Prince said. 'I'm not sure how to handle it nor what I am meant to do with it, I only know that it must be me.'

'The girl seems to know everything,' Baku said. 'She's feisty and beautiful and she scares me, to be honest.'

'She scares me too. At one time she disgusted me, and I hated her for her power and her grace and ability, but now . . .' the Prince trailed off. Those green eyes of hers were in his head; he could not shake them, or that frank, teasing look of appraisal.

'She's been gone for a while now,' Baku said, 'chasing after that bird of prey.'

'I know,' the Prince said, standing up. He went and opened the door and there was a sudden strong smell of smoke in the air, and a distant crackling sound—the sound of fire. There was a great orange glow in the sky and black smuts and gobbets of burnt wood and ash were floating down like so much black snow. The Prince was seized with panic. The forest was on fire and the wind was blowing the flames, the smoke, and the blind animal panic straight towards them. He could hear animal cries and even the horse in the lean-to was whinnying and worrying, and clattering at the wooden walls with its hooves.

He had no idea what to do. He rushed back and burst into the house, slamming open the door with a huge crash. Baku was sitting as close to the fire as he could get, trying to warm himself.

'Fire! Fire!' Osamu shouted at him, spitting and tripping over the words in his rush. 'Fire! Come on, move now!'

189

Baku stood up, confused. 'What?' he said.

'There's a huge fire from the forest. It will engulf us soon, now, at once. We must go,' the Prince shouted.

'God,' Baku said. 'What will we do without the girl? Where is she?' He thought of the ice maiden and how she might fall out of the sky and quench any fire she wanted to. How was he to perish, then, in fire or in ice? Whatever it was to be, it was getting closer.

'We have to leave,' the Prince said, running out of the room. 'The fire will destroy everything, including us.'

He rushed up the staircase into the bare room and picked up the few things he knew he must take, including those antlers from his vision of the warrior. Something had made him keep them from that first kill, and he couldn't leave them now. There seemed to be pattern and purpose to everything. The antlers were propped against his wall. The dog leapt up from the warm spot where the Prince slept, barked and ran down the stairs.

A second later the Prince heard a horse clattering up. He ran down the stairs. There was a big armoured horse in the yard with Lissa slumped across its neck. The horse shook its mane and she fell onto the ground with a cry. Her arm was exposed, and her left leg was covered in blood. Baku stood in the doorway, seemingly frozen to the spot, looking at the flames brightening the sky, so close. The Prince pushed past him and knelt beside Lissa. Her eyes were closed and he laid his head against her breast and felt the thump and rhythm of her heartbeat.

'Help me,' he said to Baku. 'We must get her inside, we haven't much time. We have to leave, and soon, or we will die. If we take her like this then she will die. What choice do we have?'

'None,' said Baku.'

Lissa lay on the table, Baku and the Prince looking down at her. The buckskin tourniquet was still tied tight on her thigh, which was covered in dried blood. The broken arrow shaft stuck up at least four inches out of her leg.

'What should we do?' the Prince said. 'She would know exactly what to do.'

'I think we should cut the leggings away from her skin and try and get the arrow out,' Baku said.

'You're right, of course,' the Prince said. 'We have almost no time, the forest is blazing. I can smell the smoke in here now.'

'We can't go anywhere with the girl like this,' Baku said.

'We can't leave her here either.'

'We must at least take out the arrowhead,' Baku said.

'How would we do that?'

'I don't know. We must cut off her clothes and see how deep it is.'

The Prince pulled the hunting knife from Lissa's belt. He took it and made a cut in the leather on her thigh near the arrowhead.

Her head rolled to one side and her clear moss eyes opened briefly, then closed again.

The Prince made a second cut down through the leather so that there was a cross cut around the arrow. He peeled back the leather like opening a fig. Then he cut quickly through the buckskin-sleeve tourniquet and threw it down onto the floor. Lissa breathed in sharply through gritted teeth and said, 'Have you cut through my leggings on this side?'

'Yes, I've made a cross cut around the arrowhead.'

She opened her eyes again and raised herself up on her elbows. She turned to Baku. 'You go out and get the horses readied as best you can, and hurry.' She coughed and closed her eyes tight, the wood smoke was drifting in now through the broken windows and black smuts were drifting down outside.

She looked down at her leg and then up at the Prince.

'Give me the knife,' she said. 'If you won't do it I must.'

'You can't,' Baku said.

'Go, Baku, leave us,' she said. 'Now.'

The Prince looked down at her bloodied leg. 'I don't want to hurt you,' he said.

'I'm already hurt. Just do it or I must. There is no time for modesty. I'm in pain.' The Prince pulled at the waist band belt and lifted her hips up slightly from the table. Lissa lifted her leg and cried out as the Prince cut all around the knee section and sloughed off the half-legging.

'Wash the blood off, quickly.'

The Prince went to the cauldron and took some warmed water. He noticed a scum of black soot was already forming on the water's surface, and he could hear the flames clearly now. He had to move fast. He hesitated, holding the goblet over her naked leg. The wound was ragged and raw-looking and inflamed, but not as large as he had feared. He cupped some water in his hands and let it trickle on to the drying blood. He held his wet hands over Lissa's leg but was afraid to touch it—it looked so ragged, like raw meat. He thought he might be sick, but somehow he would have to touch the wound.

'Clean it, then!' she screamed out through gritted teeth.

He placed his hands on her leg at once, and felt heat and also a surprising smoothness that shocked him. He had imagined that her skin might feel somehow as tough as she was herself. The delicacy and tenderness was a surprise. He stroked at her skin, carefully diluting the blood, gently washing around the wound.

'Don't be so gentle,' she said through clamped teeth. 'There is no time for that, the whole place will soon be on fire.' She looked down at the wound. 'It's all right, it's an

193

army arrow, a clean steel head and no barbs. You should be able to pull it free easily, the shoulder of the tip is at least out above my leg.'

The Prince touched the broken arrow shaft and Lissa called out. 'Aargh, no, stop, it hurts.'

He let go and stood above her, hesitating. Was her strength, her courage finally failing her?

'No time for dreaming and gawping,' she said. 'Your Highness, better give me the knife. Now take off my belt. Come on, quickly.' The Prince snapped to and undid her belt. There was an enormous crash from outside as something blazing, a tree from the sound of it, fell close by. She took the belt from him, doubled it over and put part of it in her mouth between her teeth, and bit down on it hard. She put the point of the blade just under the shoulder of the arrow head. She steadied herself, she gestured that the Prince should hold her leg still. He put his hands on her leg, one above and one below her knee. Lissa gripped the knife with both hands, closed her eyes and muttered something, a prayer the Prince supposed. Then she pulled the knife blade hard upwards.

Baku was outside with the restless horses. They had caught the scent of the fire—the air reeked of resinous burning pine, the wet sap cracked as the flames grew ever higher. He bound the two sets of reins together and tightened them, and just hoped they would hold. There were two horses between three. Baku was assuming that he would escape soon with the Prince and the girl. Thinking of the girl, he hoped he would be riding with her. He looked across to the river. The smoke was billowing out now from among the trees on their side too. Huge clouds of smoke rolled above and among the trees and the clouds were punctuated by occasional bright orange sparks. Then he heard the single scream from inside the house.

He found Lissa apparently unconscious on the table. The Prince was holding the hunting knife, a bloodied arrowhead and part of a shaft.

'She pulled it out herself,' he said.

'Ouch,' Baku said. 'I don't want to scare you further, but the flames are getting closer. We really should leave now.'

'Yes, I know,' the Prince said. 'But look at that wound. It's very nasty, and vapours and contagion will set in sooner or later unless we dress it with something: a poultice, a bandage at least, something clean.'

Masumi's travel bag was at his feet on the floor. Noticing it, Baku was reminded of something—of course!

'I have just the thing,' Baku said excitedly and he opened Masumi's travel bag and tipped the contents out. There was the blue-green moss from the side of

195

the pine tree that he had been made to gather. 'Good for wounds,' Masumi had said while they walked, that cold lifetime ago. The bundled scarf was there and also the old bronze clay mould which rolled out with a dull clatter onto the stone floor. Baku had forgotten about it.

The Prince did not notice it, and Baku quickly handed him the scarf.

'This is clean enough, and bundled in it you will find some dried moss. Put the moss next to the wound and tie the scarf round as a bandage,' Baku said. 'Master Masumi said that was what a brigand would do if he was wounded.'

'Good enough for a brigand, good enough for us. We are little more than that ourselves now,' the Prince said, then coughed as he breathed in another lungful of acrid smoke.

He washed the entry wound again. Very tenderly, because he could hardly bear to touch her, he laid the dried moss fronds across the wound. Then he asked Baku to lift her leg so that he could tie the silk square properly. He tied it tightly but also gently. He put his slender hands, palms flat, on either side of her thigh when he had finished, and he felt the warmth of her skin and the beat of her pulse.

'Put her leg down now,' the Prince said.

Baku glanced at Lissa's face in repose, at the shadow of her eyelashes on her cheek, the perfect oval of her

196

face and the fullness of her mouth. Unconscious like this she wasn't frightening at all—she reminded him of the girl he had seen just that once under the parasol in the snow. She too had been pale and tender-looking and beautiful.

'Her leg,' the Prince said.'Put it down gently.'

'Yes,' said Baku, coming to with a jolt.

Lissa's eyes swam open and closed again. Then she sat up on the table with her head held down. She coughed and her shoulders shook. She looked at the scarf bandage.'I dreamt that I was hurt,' she said,'I can't seem to feel it quite so badly now. What did you do?'

'Baku here had some medicinal moss with him and I put it next to the wound under the silk scarf.'

'Essential for wounds, my old master, Masumi, said,' Baku said, looking away and bending to the floor.

'I hope he was right,' Lissa said, slowly and carefully swinging both her legs over the edge of the table.'I can hear the fire,' she said slowly,'and I can smell it too, and it's all my fault. They might easily have followed me here.'

'Not against those flames, surely,' the Prince said. 'Careful now.' He steadied her with both hands, and she looked up and into his eyes and he looked back into hers, which were opening and closing like a child about to fall asleep.

'What would we have done without you?' she said drowsily to Baku, with her half-open eyes still held by

197

the Prince's. 'Did you bring anything else with you?'

'Well,' he said, 'there is this, I had forgotten all about it.' Baku straightened up and held the old bronze clay mould out in his hand. 'My master had it in his travel bag. I nearly buried it with him, but something made me bring it with me.' He paused: he had nearly mentioned the ice maiden, he had to be careful. Baku turned to the door, where white smoke was now curling in through the gaps. 'The fire,' he said.

Lissa sleepily held out her hand, and Baku gave her the bowl. She looked at it, turned it through her fingers at first slowly, and then her eyes widened, were fully open as she skimmed over the rusted surface. She pushed her fingers through the two holes on either side and nodded to herself; a smile split her face. A piece of folded parchment fell out.

'What's this?' she said opening it, wide awake now.

'It's a map I drew,' Baku said, hardly paying attention, noticing the signs all around of the encroaching fire. 'It shows the place where my master and his pots are buried.'

'And you nearly buried this helmet there too,' Lissa said, folding the little map and tucking it into her tunic. 'Imagine that.'

'Helmet?' said Baku. Lissa suddenly held the helmet straight up above her head in both hands. She no longer seemed fuddled by pain, but appeared to be fully alert. 'You did well not to,' she whispered. 'Here, Sire, please

198

take this from me.' She winced just a little in pain as her weight shifted, and she handed the battered bowl to the Prince.

CHAPTER TWENTY-FOUR

The Beacon

The flames had already engulfed nearly all of the trees east of the ruined house. A solid wall of fire rose up and along the route back through the forest. Clouds of birds circled and called out among the billows of acrid smoke. There was a deep-cast shadow now across the house, the garden, and the river. A daytime darkness as the black smoke mounted higher and blotted out the weak sunlight, while white smoke curled along the ground.

There was a sudden burst of intense light from inside the house. Bright beams tore out through the broken windows and pierced the ragged swirling smoke clouds in wide shafts. It was just as if a new sun had risen inside the ruined house. Shafts of light reached out through the windows and far beyond. The white light tore through the burning trees and continued in straight rays through the layers of drifting smoke as bright as its source, dazzling to the eye. At once the flames seemed diminished, as if they had been cowed by a superior force. The crackling and snapping noises fell silent, the smoke dissolved

200

away into nothingness. It was as if there had been no forest fire at all.

The Hawk-Master was struck by the light as he travelled wearily back to the army on the plain. He had given up all hope of following the girl once the flames had closed over the route she had taken. He hoped that she was dead, burned to brittle charcoal somewhere in the forest. He turned in his saddle and shielded his eyes from the intense burst of light as it rose in the sky behind him.

The Emissary too was aware of a sudden change. There was a rising noise from the gathered armies on the plain. The quality of the light had suddenly changed inside the darkened campaign tent. He stepped outside and heard the shouts and cries of the men across the fields and even the honour guard. He saw the direction of their gestures and the pointing arms. He looked up and saw great beams of white light soaring into the sky above the clouds of smoke from the distant forest fire. The beams fanned out and penetrated even higher into the sky, like a beacon, a call to arms, enough to wake the Hidden Kingdom even as he looked at them.

The Prince took the battered old bowl from Lissa and the moment his fingers touched it he felt a charge of energy shoot up his arms and through his body. And, just as with the sword, the rust, dirt, and verdigris sloughed off from the surface of the bowl until it shone and dazzled.

201

Baku turned away from it and shielded his eyes.

'Put it on your head,' Lissa said quietly.

The Prince placed the bowl on his head and the light intensified all around it like a halo. Within a second or two it surrounded his entire body. It spread from the Prince to the room then over to the windows and then all the way outside. It looked as if the light were somehow slow-moving. It was as if time itself had been slowed down to allow the forward movement of light itself to be observed. Lissa watched, astonished, as the bright silvery whiteness gradually filled the room and then travelled away from the Prince, out through the windows and into the open air.

Baku could hardly bear to look at the light. It reminded him of the vision of the ice maiden standing in front of him, just as dazzling, in the ferryman's hut that night a lifetime ago in his waking dream. He shivered and felt, if possible, even colder in the bright light of the white glare around the Prince. It was as if he had finally fulfilled all of his promises and his usefulness was now at an end, and he would fall to the ground, a useless puppet with its strings cut.

'What is it?' he asked quietly.

'We needed two things, the sword and the helmet, and you have brought them both together somehow without your knowing it. He doesn't know anything either,' Lissa said, gesturing to the Prince.

The Prince, with a puzzled expression on his face, went to take the helmet from his head.

202

'Leave it for a moment. Allow the beacon to do its job. Just let the light out.'

'What does this mean?' the Prince said.

'It means that you are sending the signal out to all the warriors of the Hidden Kingdom. You are a beacon channelling a force of energy from the helmet, and only you, the Prince Osamu, can do this. In any other mortal hands that helmet is just an ancient war helmet, battered and rusted, disguised as an old bowl, but it was forged for your line,' Lissa said. 'Your ancestor thousands of years ago wore that same helmet and wielded that same sword. You are the sole leader that can and must defeat the Emissary and his army. You are the one who must stop him bringing the demons from Hades. All the scrolls, all the scripture stories were true, all of the myths, the legends, every word that you chose to ignore.'

The light had moved away from the Prince and he stood in the shadow cast by it as it flooded the room from the outside on its slow journey upwards. He leaned back against the table, taking in what Lissa had said.

'You remind me that I am the one to fight, to lead and go to war with a demon, a supernatural being?'

'Yes it is your destiny, the destiny of your family line.'

'Why wasn't I forced to confront this before? I have been such a fool.'

'You could not be forced—you would not be told,'

Lissa said. 'You are a wilful leader, a Prince, you chose your own path and—who knows?—in the end there may be wisdom and reasoning behind those choices.'

'My master had that helmet with him,' Baku said. 'He extruded clay from it, he moulded pots using the inside of it, and Kaito had the sword hidden away, and they were both master potters.'

'They were both masters from an old school, an ancient school that trained us to be warriors as well as craftsmen. They were hidden in plain view. Some vanished completely, like Kaito, until they might be needed. Nothing is more important than to prevent the subjugation of our world by the forces of Hades.'

'When you shot that deer in the forest,' the Prince said, 'I will admit I had a vision of a warrior on a horse. I had a very strong feeling that I would see that warrior in reality. I saw him so clearly on the crest of a hill. I asked you to save the antlers from that kill didn't I?'

'You did,' Lissa said. 'They are upstairs leaning against the wall in my room.' She turned to Baku. 'Would you fetch the antlers, please?'

'No,' the Prince said, 'I have them here already, I was going to take them with me, because of the fire.' The Prince turned to the door. There was no longer any smoke curling around the hinges and under the sill.

'Have you noticed something?' Lissa said.

'I have,' the Prince nodded.

'What?' asked Baku.

'The fire has stopped, burned itself out. The beacon light has finished it.'

'So it has,' Baku said. 'How is that possible?'

'Many things are possible now. They will have seen the beacon.'

'Who will have seen it?'

'The army that you mentioned,' Lissa said, 'the one waiting on the plain, they will attack now.'

'The rational part of me cannot accept any of this,' the Prince said. 'And yet I have seen things with my own eyes.' And he reached forward and picked the sword up from the table. The energy in the sword ran up his arms at once. 'And I feel it now,' he added, 'more strongly too.'

Lissa took up the antlers and asked the Prince for the helmet. She fitted an antler into each of the holes in the gleaming metal. At once the metal, as if it were suddenly liquid, swirled and fused around the antlers as if it had been waiting for them to be fitted. The antlers then fused with the metal so that they appeared to be made of silver instead of horn.

Lissa put the helm back onto the Prince's head. 'There,' she said. 'You were the warrior you saw, it was all for a reason.'

'I wish I understood the reason. How does your wound feel,' he said looking down at her bound thigh.

'Painful,' she said, 'what else?'

'What should we do now?' Baku asked.

205

'Now we go,' Lissa said. 'The beacon shines, they will come to us now.'

'Who will come?' the Prince said. 'And where will we go?'

'Your army, the army of the Hidden Kingdom, the ones who have waited for the sign, will come and we must go and meet them. We will follow the beacon like them. See how the light is moving.'

It was true—the intense light was high in the sky now like a comet and slowly moving away.

'The horses are ready outside,' Baku said.

'We'll take the dog with us,' the Prince said.

'That is your choice,' Lissa said.

'Yes, it is,' the Prince said firmly. Their eyes locked again and he was sure that she was about to say something scathing, that they should leave the dog to its fate, but she didn't. She smiled instead.

'Just as I once said, dogs just *are*, they *love*,' she said. 'You are learning, Your Highness.'

The Prince put the sword down and called out to the dog. The dog came and nuzzled its head against his hand and the Prince ruffled its ears.

'I have no armour and you are wounded, how are we supposed to lead an army?'

'The Kingdom will provide,' Lissa said, 'I feel less pain now and I can ride double with you. I can shoot. We will prevail, we must prevail.'

Baku said, 'I will do my best to help, although without

that sword I doubt I will be of much use to anyone,' and he shivered, holding his cold hands out to the guttering fire.

'You could start by putting one of the bedding cloths on the back of a horse, because two of us will need to double up on one of them,' Lissa said to Baku, 'choose the bigger horse.'

Lissa slipped off from the edge of the table. The Prince stepped forward and took her weight in his arms.

'If you ride behind me you can hold on to me and stay warm.'

The Prince let go of Lissa and fetched down the white snow coat she had stripped from the brigand in the forest. 'Here,' he said. 'Wear this now, it will help.' And he wrapped the heavy coat carefully around her shoulders. She let go of him for a moment and he put first one arm through a sleeve and then the other. He pulled her back, closer to him, and she lifted her head and he looked down into her eyes. She closed them then and stayed still with her head tilted up. The Prince felt compelled to lower his mouth towards hers. And then Baku came in.

'Sorry,' he said. He looked at them, close-wrapped together in the rough white fur of the brigand's coat, almost kissing, and he closed his eyes for a moment. He felt what was left of his poor pierced heart break and shatter like thin ice. When he had seen Lissa for the first time he had recognized at once that here was a fierce mortal equal in beauty to his ice maiden, a humble girl, brave and resourceful, a fit companion to a master potter perhaps. And real, too, tangible flesh and blood, not a remote goddess, not a demon living in the sky. He could suddenly see all too clearly the emotion and pull between Lissa and the Prince. He should have realized it sooner. He had no one left to dream of now except the ice maiden, the white demon, whatever and whoever she was. No one was more beautiful than her and what's more she was his own, she was his sworn secret. No one knew about her, no one could know, and he would not, could not, tell them. The thought of her beautiful cold embrace was the only thing left that might actually warm him through. And when would that happen? 'Never,' he muttered, and then said out loud, 'The horses are ready. And you were right, there's smoke but no fire.' Then he thought, Except between you two.

CHAPTER TWENTY-FIVE

The Hidden Kingdom

In the yard outside a thick white mist drifted everywhere and there was a strong smell of wood smoke and pine resin. The horses were calm and Lissa was lifted into the military saddle by Baku and the Prince. When the Prince mounted she clasped him tightly around the waist and rested her head against his back.

The light was now a daytime comet in the sky, bright and still moving, sending down great shafts of light through the smoke.

'Just follow it,' Lissa said, tightening her grip on the Prince.

They rode out and away from the drifting smoke. At first they took the roadway through the remaining trees. It was as if the light beams were walking ahead of them. The long shafts of bright light pierced the mist like long legs reaching from the sky and just touching the bare ground.

A rider appeared out of the trees at the side of the road. Lissa sat up, alert, and pulled the bow from her back. As they approached the rider dismounted, knelt on

209

the ground and bowed his head. From behind some trees two other figures appeared and they too prostrated themselves as the Prince approached. They were holding spears which looked homemade, kitchen knives or cleavers lashed onto long bamboo poles with rope.

'What's going on?' the Prince asked.

'This will be the leading edge of your army, the army of the Hidden Kingdom,' Lissa said. 'They have been summoned by the light. They will have been waiting, some of them, all of their lives to respond to the beacon, the light in the sky. I think we will discover more and more of them as we go.'

Baku had turned in his saddle. 'Look behind,' he said.

There was already a build-up behind them, a line of riders and walkers, with more spilling out of the trees and falling in line as they rode.

'It's all true then,' the Prince said. 'Just look at them.'

'Of course it's true,' Lissa said.

After an hour or so of riding the Prince found himself at the head of a real army. The trail of willing volunteers, the hidden army of the Hidden Kingdom stretched in a long line behind them on the road. There were riders, wagons, farmers with improvised weapons, warriors—both men and women, young and old—all, it seemed, had emerged at the signal of the light in the sky. The numbers were growing by the minute.

The Prince rode on as the sky darkened around the glittering bright comet and the day waned. Lissa's arms were tight around his waist all the time now, which felt suddenly so right. Baku rode beside them and the dog trotted beside Baku. When the sky itself was dark, even though the light from the comet enabled them to see the road ahead, the Prince pulled the horse over into the trees. He stood and looked back down the road. Camp fires had already sprung up dotted along the sides of the road. It seemed that the Prince's army had realized it was time to rest too and had all stopped just before he had.

Baku set to work and soon had a fire going, anything to try and get warm. It was not long before a delegation from the hidden army arrived. There were two of them, an armoured warrior and a shorter, older man who was carrying a basket on his head. They both bowed to the Prince. Lissa was sitting propped against a tree close to the fire.

The armoured warrior stepped forward.

'Sire,' he said, 'if I may present myself and my companion. I am called Hiroshi. Once, long ago, I was a soldier, then a farmer and now I hope I may be a soldier again. This brave man, Kazuki, is my neighbour and a fine farmer,' he said indicating the man with the basket. 'He has food for you. We are here to serve.'

'Welcome, General Hiroshi. Lissa, my companion is hurt. It was an arrow injury. Do you know of any medical men among the army?'

'I am sure we can find one, and soon, Your Majesty.'

'Good,' the Prince said. 'This girl is precious to me.'

'Understood,' said Hiroshi with a bow.

They sat by the fire and ate Kazuki's cold roasted partridge and rice. Kazuki went back down the line and was soon back. He bowed to the Prince. 'This, Majesty, is Yoshio, a doctor of medicine and herbs.'

Yoshio bowed too and then set to work and re-bandaged Lissa's wound.

'Whoever dressed this wound did the right thing,' he said.

The sound of singing rose up from all around them among the fires and the cooking smells. It was impossible to tell how many had been summoned by the light, but the glow of the camp fires stretched all the way back to the far distance. The singing was not mournful, not the kind of singing you might expect on the eve of possible battle. It was joyous, as if the whole of the army around them were on some extended holiday jaunt.

After they had eaten Hiroshi leaned across and reached towards the sword. He looked to the Prince, who gave a brief nod of permission. Hiroshi touched the sword. He closed his eyes as if he might be feeling the energy.

'It is as if that ancient sword were speaking to me,' he said, 'telling me its history. I can feel its power and its age. It is all here—the history is fused into the very fabric of the metal itself.'

'When I hold it I feel only its power surging through me, as if I were channelling a form of lightning,' the Prince said.

'In a way that is what you *are* doing,' Hiroshi said. Then he stood up. 'We shall leave you to rest now. The light will watch over us but we must be ready. The dawn will bring our destiny.'

'Wait,' the Prince said. 'I have not even a thought in my head of a plan or a battle strategy. You are an old soldier, will you help me?'

'I should be honoured to try. There are other old hands among us here—I will rally them and we will come to you at dawn. In the meantime you must rest, we all must.'

He bowed, as did the others. It reminded the Prince a little of how his life used to be back in the palace. There he had the same deference but no fear, no sense of over-whelming responsibility. Nothing had been expected of him other than to be himself. He had written his poetry, admired his pots, and appreciated the beauty around him in the way of a small child gazing in wonder on a field of wild flowers.

Now it was different. He was out under the trees, surrounded by a whole ragged but determined army, who had been drawn from every corner of his king-dom and were looking to him as their leader. They were expecting him to save their world from something dark and foul, an evil which he could not even imagine. Some species of slime, sickening matter that had crawled free from Hades itself, was caged in armour and bent on laying waste the earth in advance of its demon masters and their arrival. This had all happened once before, thousands of years before, a period of time for a demon like the blink of a mortal eye. Somehow, he, Osamu the poet prince, was expected to defeat an army led by this creature, this dark shadow.

Well, donning the helmet had brought the comet light, had rallied the Hidden Kingdom to his side, perhaps other wonders would reveal themselves with the dawn? His moment would come. He lacked knowledge and fighting skills but was fierce in his sudden love for Lissa, who had skills to spare, and for Baku the sword messenger, and for his people, and not least for his loyal dog. He had heard the voices singing on the night air, he would do his best until death and no one could ask anything more of him.

Baku stroked the dog's ears. He looked over at Lissa, who had fallen asleep. Her beautiful head was propped inside the folded white coat. The singing had died down too, and gradually the fires had been put out and a kind of moonlit silver darkness had descended over the trees. He heard an owl call. He felt frozen inside and out. The cold was getting worse, even though the snow was mostly gone he felt colder than ever. He thought that even if he were to lie down beside Lissa, all curled into the white fur of her coat, he would still feel like a man drowning slowly in an icy river.

The Prince nodded to him and then went and lay next to Lissa. The sword and helmet were on the ground beside him. It seemed to Baku that the Prince fell asleep at once, his arms tight around the girl. Their two dark heads together on the pillow of white fur, which looked as soft as a cloud. He could see their two profiles one beside the other. The shadow of Lissa's lashes on her cheek were matched by the Prince's own. They looked suddenly like the perfect couple, moulded together as if they had always been intended as companions one for the other: a natural king and his queen. Baku wondered why he had even for moment harboured the thought that Lissa might be the one for him, his companion, the dutiful wife of a potter. No, she was meant for Osamu, meant by the gods who ordered the clockwork of the universe. What had his old master Masumi said to him that night in the ferryman's hut?

'It was one of those nights, Baku, when everything seems to be in place, when the mysterious gods who work our universe have moved everything to be in your favour, and, believe me, you had better recognize that time when and if it happens to you.'

Of course, Baku felt a surge of real happiness for them, a brief burst of elation shivered through his cold frame. He had recognized just such a moment in his own destiny. Lissa was not for him, he loved only one

215

person. He closed his eyes and he saw at once the face of the ice maiden leaning towards him, he could feel her finger on his lips and it felt warm. Whenever he pictured her she smiled at him, she welcomed him. He had told no one about her. He had kept his dream promise. He prayed to her now for help in what was about to happen. Baku, unlike the Prince, had seen the armies on the plain. He had seen the scale of the battle to come. Inwardly he vowed to protect the Prince and Lissa, whatever the cost.

The Prince was conscious of the welcome weight of Lissa's head as it slipped and nestled onto his shoulder after he had settled next to her. He could smell her hair. It had a beautiful, dark oily smell which was overlaid with the smell of sweet clover and also the smell of the earth itself and the resinous tree roots. Lissa's warm body was next to him, they were lying together on the good earth of his kingdom, the Hidden Kingdom, and all around them were slumped and sleeping figures. Each one was summoned by the light and each one, it seemed, was willing to die for that same earth and that same place.

He looked up through the branches of the tall pines. He could see the stars, the patterns of constellations, the bright pinpoints of heaven piercing the black. There was a cold mist swirling through the branches, which looked like faintly glittering crystals of ice as it caught the faint light from the stars.

Baku thought that he could see her face up among the drifting ice crystals. The face of his love, the face of the ice maiden. He hoped he knew what it meant. He hoped that when the beautiful pale face in the mist looked down on him, sprawled and freezing under layers of saddle blankets, that it was her true face, and that she was looking down on him with favour. He hoped that she had come to help him and that she would rise up again in a whirl of ice as she had done before. That he might soon see her again and even feel that longed-for touch of her cold finger on his lips.

CHAPTER TWENTY-SIX

The Morning

The Prince woke before light. Lissa's head was still resting on his shoulder. He could hear the stirrings of his hidden army. The clattering of cooking pots and murmurs of hushed conversation drifted among the trees. He kissed Lissa on the forehead and her fringe of dark hair tickled his nose. She opened her eyes sleepily and he looked into them, into the mossy grey-green colour. He marvelled at the skin of her forehead and around her eyes, which was almost all that was visible, the rest of her face tucked into the white fur collar of the brigand's coat. Her skin was as smooth as marble or alabaster, or a particularly refined porcelain finish. Unlike his pots she was a living thing, vibrant and contrary. She was violent and fearless, and he was touched by the thought that her whole life had been built around the idea of protecting him, when and if she had to. He supposed that whole generations had come and gone in the Hidden Kingdom dedicated to that same principle of protective sacrifice. That whole lives had been spent waiting just in case the worst should happen, that the summons would come. Now it had, and it fell to Lissa and to himself to act to save everything and themselves. If they succeeded he determined that they would be together in every sense.

He gently moved her head back on to the fur pillow and pulled himself up. The whole encampment was stirring. The sledge dog pattered over to him and the Prince stroked its head. The sword was already strapped at his side and he decided to carry the antlered helmet under his arm.

He set off to walk among his hidden army.

Breakfasts were being taken or cooked among the dense trees all around. He could see the smoke rising from a thousand small fires and he could smell cooking fish and meat. Men were busily shining their swords, polishing and preparing their weapons, their bows and arrows, axes, and cudgels. The Prince noticed the number and range of homemade weapons. He saw a scythe being sharpened as if the owner were intending to cut down a whole field of soldiers like so much wheat.

All bowed solemnly or inclined their heads as he passed by them with the dog at his side.

The forest ended on a rise and there was a drop down to the flat plain. Below him was a gentle slope of scrubland littered with old rotting timber. Hiroshi caught up with the Prince. He had several older soldiers with him and

219

they all had a snatched breakfast together overlooking the wide plain beyond the last line of trees. The area of flat, cold ground stretched far away to the horizon and was lit by the comet, which had stabilized and hovered in the middle of the sky. Hiroshi introduced each of the soldiers in turn, and each of them bowed and touched the helmet.

Hiroshi signed to the Prince that they might go forward a little further down the slope away from the trees. The Prince and the soldiers stepped down the slope, across mounds of discarded branches and rotting logs, until they stood together in the space the below the tree line at the edge of the plain. Hiroshi took the Prince a little further off.

'Each of these men I have brought to you,' he said, resting his hand on the Prince's shoulder, 'has experience in battle, or knowledge of weapons and tactics. Each is as brave as a lion.'

'Thank you, Hiroshi,' the Prince said. 'Would you mind if I appointed you as my general?'

'I should be honoured, Sire.'

'Good. Use the men you have chosen as you see best. As I have said, my skills and knowledge extend only to poetry.'

'That may be, Sire, but you wear the helmet, you raise the sword, it is you who will lead us. It is meant to be this way.'

'I will do my best until death, General Hiroshi.'

220

Hiroshi bowed low, and went back to his men, leaving the Prince to look out over the plain.

There was nothing to see as yet but the flat stretch of shabby grassland reaching back as far as the horizon. It seemed clear that the terrible place of battle had been chosen. The Prince looked over at the flat fields stretching away in front of him, and it was as if something had suddenly clutched and torn at his heart with icy fingers. His soul was filled suddenly with an all-enveloping sense of dread and evil. As if the whole of the flat, nondescript landscape in front of them was pervaded and watched over by something unspeakable. Something filled with a real sense of deep hatred for all mankind. The Prince shivered and forced himself to turn away from the horrible flat emptiness.

His spirits rose a little because Lissa was coming towards him down the slope. She was being helped down by Baku, supporting herself on an improvised crutch of pine branch. She was soon beside him. They stood together and watched as a sudden shadow darkened the far side of the plain.

'Oh no, oh God, look there they are,' Baku said, pointing across the plain. He recognized the narrow white banners fluttering in the far distance. What could have been weapons flashed bright metallic reflections across from the other side. And there was a sound too, the low thunderous rumble, the stamp of marching feet.

Lissa could feel Baku shivering and trembling next

to her. She looked at Osamu the Prince, and it was as if the colour had drained completely from his face, he was ashen.

'Soon it will begin,' he said, turning to her, pale and frightened-looking. For the first time in a long time he looked young again, like a scared boy.

Hiroshi suggested that they climbed the slope back under the shelter of the trees. Once safely hidden he raised a brass telescope and trained it on the enemy lines, then he turned to Osamu, bowed, and handed the telescope to him.

'Look upon the enemy, Sire, it will help. We must prevail, and we will, however hopeless it may look now. We are united together against this evil darkness. Many of us have waited half our lifetimes in case this threat rose up again in our generation. We will fight to the last man, woman or child, the stakes are that high. We may be a disparate group in ages and skills but the enemy is a cynical mess of hack mercenaries and demon-worshippers. Even from here I see many jostling allegiances, clashing banners and flags. Half of them will have no idea what they are fighting for, and the others will be doing so out of coercion, threat, misguided belief in the supremacy of evil, or just the money. This is an essential weakness. We are committed to our cause, which is the survival of everything mortals hold dear, our earthly world and everything in it. And we shall prevail through our faith in you and in humanity itself.'

The Prince lowered the telescope.

'There are so many of them,' he said in a quiet and shocked voice.

'There are equal numbers on our side,' Hiroshi said. 'It is time to be ready to summon ourselves to arms, with your permission, Sire?'

The Prince nodded and then lowered his head and looked at the earth at his feet. He reached out for Lissa's hand, and he took it in both of his. She could feel him trembling.

'Look at me,' she said. The Prince looked directly into her eyes. 'I will be with you, I will watch you every inch of the way. You know what you must do. I am as scared as you are. You owe it to all of the people around us and behind us to betray nothing of your fear to them.'

'You are right,' the Prince said. 'I shall at least give the appearance of courage.' He turned to Hiroshi. 'Sound the call,' he said.

Hiroshi gestured to an armoured bandsman who raised a hunting horn and blasted out a loud rallying call which echoed back through the trees.

The hidden army was soon assembled in neat long ranks. The armoured forces were at the front all along the shadow of the tree line. They stayed in place where they were while the dark army marched across the distant plain towards them. Dawn had passed, leaving the sky a heart-meltingly pretty blue, which the Prince noticed with a pang. Perhaps this would be the last such sky any of them would ever see?

The Prince had once seen a vision of a warrior on the rise of just such a hill wearing a helmet pierced with antlers. He realized that once he raised his helmet onto his own head his vision would be fulfilled and complete. He also knew that the moment he lifted the helmet to his head something dramatic would happen.

He hesitated and looked round. Lissa was now mounted on a horse next to him, her bow ready in her hands, a quiver stuffed full of arrows across her shoulders. Baku was on a horse too. He had been given a sword by somebody and was now wearing some odd scraps of borrowed armour. Hiroshi sat mounted on his left side watching the approaching army. He knew the stakes only too well. If the mercenaries won the day then the seven demons would be released into the world, the seven demons that ruled over Hades, and everything in this world would be changed for ever. The beauties of the world would disappear, all men would be slaves, all values would be turned upside down. It would mean the death of love and beauty and of everything else too. It simply could not be allowed to happen.

The Prince said, 'I have led you all to disaster. I have nothing that can help. I have no knowledge or experience in battle. I have never fought anyone or anything. I have no strategy. I have no plan, I can offer nothing to all of these brave people who have been summoned here. I am no one, and certainly not a warrior: I am an amateur of pots, a writer of self-indulgent verses. I have nothing that you or anyone else should put your faith in.'

'On the contrary, you most certainly do,' Hiroshi said. 'Lift up your helmet, Sire, and put it on your head.'

The Prince lifted the silvery helmet with its glittering antlers up onto his head.

The Hawk-Master rode next to the Emissary and his outriders. The Emissary was hidden inside a canopy mounted on the back of an enormous black horse. They rode in a phalanx in the centre of the army.

The army marched with weapons ready-drawn. The armoured divisions marched stamping their iron-shod feet down in deadly sounding, regular thumps, bass drum-beats that made the ground tremble. It seemed that the earth might split open and spill the contents of the underworld, spew Hades itself out like volcanic lava and cover everything with fire and darkness— which was what would happen if they finally won the battle.

There was the problem of the Prince, of course. The Prince was meant to be dead already, or at least separated from his sword and helmet. The Emissary had not been pleased by that outcome.

225

It was then that the mysterious and troubling light in the sky suddenly brightened so that all were dazzled for a moment. The comet was now brighter than the sun. The Hawk-Master could no longer see the signs of the hidden army along the tree line. He did not see them as they emerged from the shadow of the forest.

Something fell from the sky with a searing whistling sound. He heard an arrow thump into the body of a soldier a few lines ahead of them. Cries went up from the ranks, screams and shouts filled the air as arrows found their mark. The archers of the Hidden Kingdom fired volley after volley out of the dazzling light and into the ranks of the blinded mercenary army.

The cry went up, 'Raise your shields!' and all the way down the line the conscripted armies blocked the arrows and some shafts of the dazzling light with their shields. The Hawk-Master could already see riderless horses rearing among the mounted men and scattered bodies among the ranks of the infantry, who all moved forward without breaking step, such was the hold and power of the Emissary.

Hiroshi turned to the Prince. 'See here, Sire, through my lens, in the centre of the cavalry.'

The Prince took the glass from Hiroshi and scanned the ranks of mounted riders. There in the centre was a huge black farmhorse supporting a shadowy canopy of black cloth, which was closed and drawn to.

'I see it,' the Prince said.

'That is your target, Sire. That is the Emissary, the demon who controls that whole army. Armies, I should say.'

'What must I do?'

'Get close and destroy it. You have the sword and are the only one who can.'

The Prince turned to Lissa. 'I have seen my target. Hiroshi will sound the charge and I must go forward with the sword raised.'

'I know,' Lissa said.

'I may never see you again.'

'I know that.'

'I . . .' he hesitated, unsure how to utter the words he had never spoken to anyone ever before.

'Go on,' she said.

'I love you, Lissa.'

'I know that too.'

The thunderous noise of the approaching army continued and the hidden archers fired volley after volley out of the bright light and into the armoured ranks. At the same time the Prince ordered a blast on the horn. Without turning to Lissa or Baku, he raised his sword. In his head the Prince had that same vision he had had once before of the helmeted warrior, sword raised, about

227

to descend a slope at the head of an army, and now he could see all too clearly that it was himself. The sword crackled with energy and the metal shimmered, and he felt the charge of power, as if taken directly from the light in the sky, travel through his body. He was lit up and surrounded by a dazzle of light as he rode forward down the slope and out onto the flat plain. He heard the rush of hooves flowing close behind him and the slow rhythmic stamp of the marching army in front of him across the brightly lit fields. His horse seemed as energized as he was, and part of him was watching everything as if outside himself. He could not believe that he was on a charging horse with a sword raised in anger and heading straight for serried ranks of warriors, all of whom meant him harm. He could smell the wet earth and the cold air. He was conscious of gripping onto the reins with one hand and of the very light weight of the sword in the other. He had no real intention of striking out at anyone, of really using the sword. It was a fine, early spring morning on the good earth—how could he even think of striking at anyone with a sharp sword?

He was so close to the invading army that he had to make a choice. He headed for the centre of the line and carried on forwards. He passed through the first two lines of soldiers and then struck out instinctively with the sword. He felt contacts and he heard cries and saw arcs and spatters of blood spray in the air very slowly as he passed through. Whether he had caused the blood or

228

the arrows that flew past him with a shrieking buzz over the cries, he had no idea. He was fixed only on finding the black horse and the shadowy black canopy. Warriors aimed blows at him, but nothing seemed to touch him. He heard the rising cries and roars of battle behind him in his wake, but he did not, could not look back for fear of losing his momentum.

His head was full of the sound of battle now, the clash and clang of metal on metal, the speeded-up hornet buzz of arrows, the shouts and the cries, and the screaming of horses. It was not long before his own horse was cut from under him. The horse went down onto the wet red mud of the plain almost silently. He watched its front legs scrabble in the air and then he was down, flat on his back. He propped himself up in time to see a foot soldier standing over him holding a double-headed axe. Without thought the Prince leapt up and swung the sword. He sliced the axe head clean away from the stout handle. He did not wait to see the reaction but finished the soldier off with one blow, hardly noticing the man as he fell forward.

The Prince moved off, dodging swords and axes. His senses were sharpened now and everything appeared to be happening very slowly. He could track the flight of the arrows, which were still being fired in volleys from behind him. He could watch them as they passed slowly overhead and landed with exaggerated thunks into the chest or head of an enemy soldier. The Prince took no pleasure in it all. He was only really conscious of two things: the ephemeral beauty of the day itself, which was somehow tied up with the beauty of the sacrifice that was being made all around him by his hidden army, and the need to find the Emissary.

He couldn't have said how many times he swung the sword or how many fell as a result of the movement of his arms. He was like Kazuki the farmer with his scythe for a weapon: he was cutting down the enemy like so many stalks of wheat. His arm and his aim were unerring. Not only were the movements around him slowed but the sounds went quiet too. The Prince was in his own pocket of sound and movement. Occasionally his sword would snag against the thrust of a particularly strong arm or an extra thickness of armour and he had to double the blow or the speed of the blow so that he was sure he must have blurred like a phantom. His path through the battle was littered with corpses and with cleanly severed limbs. He felt no fear and no real disgust at what he was doing, that might come later, but now he had a task, and no task had ever been more important. His mind was almost emptied of everything but that necessity of the destruction of the Emissary and his army.

There was Lissa, of course, and there was a part of him was hollow with terror at the thought that something might happen to her. Lissa was brave and resourceful, she was trained as a fighter, was accurate with a bow, and her injury would not stop her. She would be covering his back following every move, but the Prince did not turn around once in his movement forwards across the plain towards the shadow of the Emissary.

Lissa was indeed hard behind the Prince and Baku was hard behind her. She had galloped after Osamu as soon as he rode off recklessly down the slope onto the plain. She watched his progress through the fierce ranks of warriors, slicing, parrying—nothing stopped him until the moment when his horse was shot out from under him. She used her arrows then, and she caught a warrior in the throat with one shot fired from low in the saddle as her horse galloped. She had given Baku the pistol that she had stolen from the brigand but so far he had not used it.

Baku felt a little safer now that he was wearing some hastily donated scraps of armour, which he had pulled on over his apprentice's tunic. He kept one hand on the butt of the pistol as he rode. He had never seen anything like the battle that was being played out all around him. Lissa was fearless, despite her injury. She was riding fast behind the Prince, dispatching warriors in his wake with her arrows. Horses were falling all around, twisting as they fell, collapsing and trapping their riders under them. Warriors were deliberately aiming at the horses, slashing at their legs or splitting them open with swords from underneath. It was a horrible business. Baku felt, if anything, even colder than he had been feeling for the last few days. He was an ice man now, controlled and steely and able to look at things that would have normally sent him screaming and running as far away as he could. His hand tightened on the pistol. He was sure there would come a moment when he would need it.

The Hawk-Master watched the progress of the Prince through the ranks of soldiers. He saw men slaughtered at speed, saw the fountains of blood and the oddly blurred movements of the Prince moving and killing as if safe inside a hard bubble of enchantment. He ordered an archer to fire on the Prince's horse. The first arrow missed. The second found its mark and he saw the silver figure fall with his horse among the troops and the bloodied mud. He spurred his own horse onwards to where the Prince had fallen: this would be his chance. As he got nearer he saw a girl with a long dark plait of hair mounted low on a stolen military horse. She was following the Prince, zigzagging behind him, firing arrows from low in the saddle. It was the same girl, the one who had killed his men, the girl who had so carelessly and with a single arrow despatched his familiar, his seeker, his beloved hooded hawk. So, she was the Prince's defender too? Well, he surely had her now. He levelled his long-barrelled fouling piece and pulled back the hammer. He just needed her to rise up in the saddle.

CHAPTER TWENTY-SEVEN
Loss and Death on The Plain

The Prince made off on foot towards the shadow that was the Emissary. He moved unnaturally fast across the ground, impelled by the energy of the sword and his need to finish the horror of battle as soon as he could. He held the sword above his head in both hands, whirling and slashing with it as he ran, oblivious of anything except the strange shadowy area where the canopy rode unsteadily on the back of the big black horse.

Lissa rode behind him, her injured thigh pressed painfully against the flank of the horse. Baku rode just beside her and his eyes scanned the ranks like a bird of prey as they passed through the melee, looking for any danger, however distant.

It was then that the ice cloud formed near him. The crystals descended, flashing and catching light from the comet above in the blue sky. The white shape was like an icy river running suddenly through the battle at head height. The river of ice swirled and formed suddenly into her, the ice maiden. Baku could see her hair flowing out as a dark space among the flow of white, and then her

234

beautiful dark eyes dazzled him for a moment. Then he saw her arm extend out and she pointed across the field with her finger, the finger that had touched him, and he longed for that touch again. He looked to see where she was pointing. He saw as if haloed in white light an enemy warrior on a big horse holding a long-barrelled weapon tucked against his shoulder. Time itself slowed then for Baku: he clearly saw the warrior pull back the hammer and cock the weapon ready to fire. He also saw that the weapon was pointing directly at Lissa. The eyes of the ice maiden bore into him. He knew exactly what he had to do.

Lissa could hardly keep up with the Prince. She was aware of every dodge and move he made, running through the maelstrom of blades and arrows. She kept low in her saddle for the most part, not wishing to present a tall target to any archer or swordsman. Then she noticed a rider gaining on the running Prince from a way ahead of him. She gestured to Baku, but he was looking in another direction, so she straightened up in the saddle, pulled an arrow from her quiver and aimed her bow.

The Hawk-Master was balanced and waiting for the girl to rise up. He squeezed the trigger of his weapon. His aim was true.

* * *

Baku clearly saw the puff of misted smoke as it drifted with an agonizing slowness out of the octagonal barrel of the weapon. He spurred his horse level with Lissa. He saw the sudden flash of percussive fire bright against the smoke. He saw something else too, bright like a line of quicksilver, a spinning dot of shining metal heading through the air and he heard the gun roar like a black bear. He steadied himself and as the silvery bullet approached he stood up tall in the saddle and turned to face it, willing it on towards him. He was aware too of the ice maiden floating nearer with her arms wide. He knew many things in that slow instant of time as the bullet neared him. He knew that he loved the ice maiden just as his master, Masumi, had done. That his master had openly acknowledged his love by telling Baku, and that was why she had appeared and taken him at once with a kiss. Baku knew that he loved her and that she loved him, that she was many things, and that among them she was a merciful death, a protector of man, and the end of suffering. He rose up as high as he could in the saddle. In that eternal instant of time Baku knew now why he had been so cold since that night in the ferryman's hut. He too had died that night. She had chosen him, had bestowed her beauty on him and he had kept her secret, had remained true. He had been one of the walking dead ever since. Now it was time for him to join his love in eternity and sacrifice himself for the love of the Prince and Lissa. He greeted the spinning bullet when it finally arrived with a smile even as it shattered his skull and tore his fragile head apart, as Lissa fired the arrow that saved the Prince.

Lissa felt the hot rush of blood across her face and turned in time to see Baku slump back in his saddle. She called out, 'Baku!' and jerked her horse to a sudden halt. Baku's body fell from his saddle. Lissa jumped down and supported him but one glance at his shattered head was enough to tell her that he was dead.

'Poor Baku,' she said; his body felt suddenly and surprisingly warm. Unseen by Lissa until it was upon her, a rush of icy air had swept across the terrible plain in a cloud of sparking ice grains, a pair of beautiful pale arms cradled Baku's soul, and he felt the first real rush of warmth and love course through him it seemed for an age, as he was kissed and his soul melted into the ice maiden's. Lissa saw her for an instant among the ice crystals, saw her beautiful sad eyes and the sweep of her night-black hair and watched as her mouth closed on Baku's and kissed him. Then the ice maiden turned and spiralled through the air back towards the Hawk-Master.

He had watched appalled as his special bullet missed its mark and blew apart the head of some witless anonymous grunt, a mounted soldier, instead. He had watched the girl fire her arrow and watched as yet another of his fine warriors fell from his horse with an arrow sticking out of his neck.

The girl had stopped to help the soldier. Now he

237

watched her get back in her saddle, and she swerved off again after the Prince, who was in turn now dangerously close to the Emissary. The Hawk-Master, without even reloading, spurred his own horse on to head her off. He cut through the ranks, carelessly trampling soldiers on both sides as he thundered at a diagonal towards the Prince. A swirl of white ice crystals rose up from the ground like a whirlwind, right in front of him. His horse reared up on its hind legs, and the Hawk-Master dropped his weapon and fell onto his back on the ground, his fish-scale armour making a bone-shaking clatter and crash. He struggled to get up. He had managed to get onto his elbows when an elderly figure dressed in no armour at all, just the simple quilted cottons of a peasant farmer, stepped in front of him. The Hawk-Master scrabbled for the gun, cocked it and managed to raise it. He pulled the trigger but the hammer fell with a harmless click. The farmer Kazuki stamped at once on the Hawk-Master's arm, pinning him to the ground.

'Get your filthy foot off me, you peasant,' the Hawk-Master shouted out, struggling to free himself. It was the last thing he said. Kazuki raised his old and sharply honed scythe and cut through the Hawk-Master's throat and neck just below the helmet line, with the practised ease of a man who had scythed whole rolling fields of wheat in less than an afternoon. The farmer Kazuki took no more notice of the Hawk-Master's surprised head bouncing off across the field of battle

238

than he would the destruction of a twisted stand of unwelcome weeds.

The Prince ran on across the field. He had lost count, if he had ever even noticed, of how many had fallen as the result of his sword arm. He waved and flailed it two-handed as he ran on, impervious to everything around him. He sliced and chopped and struck out with the sword on all sides, cutting a path over to the shadowed area where the Emissary waited.

The Emissary watched the tide and flow of battle from behind his black iron mask. His armour had been specially forged for him by a demon in a lake of hell fire. He could see everything through the partings in the heavy, smoke-black curtains that surrounded him. Every spray or trace of spilled blood made his dark heart sing. Every life that suddenly ended in a horrible wound added to his strength and certainty, from whichever side the victim favoured. The more death and horror that surrounded him the more his twisted spirit lifted and soared. The very sound of the battle was like music to him. The screams of the dying, the anguished cries of the torn and disembowelled horses, the ugly clash of metal on metal, or the sounds of iron and steel as they bit hacked and sliced into soft human flesh.

He was, however, only too aware of the survival of the Prince Osamu, the antler helmeted young fool. He was the only threat to the Emissary across the whole hideous and blasted plain. At some point he knew that the boy would confront him and he would have to be ready. He lurched forwards across the black cushions. He eased what passed for his legs down from the saddle of the silent horse that supported him and stepped outside the canopy for the first time since the battle had started. His honour guards flinched and shied away from his shadowed presence. They were human, after all, and even to see him half-hidden by his protective armour was a distressing enough sight.

They soon recovered and formed an orderly phalanx around him, their bannered lances raised out horizontally on all sides as if they were suddenly one single armoured creature, a porcupine, bristling with lethal spines.

The Emissary sensed at once the loss of the Hawk-Master. He could trace the path of the freshly severed head in the tunnels of his vast, dark imagination. He was able to watch it as it rolled around amongst the armoured feet of the battle-weary soldiers, kicked around like a football. The progress of the Hawk-Master's severed head caused what passed for a face at the front of the Emissary's own head to attempt a smile.

Somewhere else in the twisted mind of the Emissary was the knowledge that with the Hawk-Master gone he was more vulnerable to attack, that his tactician and adviser was gone now, and however comical the manner of his passing, it represented some real danger to the whole project. He stood to his full height so that his clouded black cloak fell around him. He carried no weapon—he had no need of one, after all he was a weapon in his being. His honour guards steadied themselves, happy to be facing outwards, away from him. The Emissary made out two particular figures on the field of battle. First was a young woman on a horse, she was an archer and she rode fast and fired at the same time and she was heading in his direction. She was obviously a skilful rider—she was controlling the horse using her legs—and he also sensed her injury on the wind. He savoured it like a special perfume of hurt. She was keeping pace with, and riding just behind the Prince in his antlered helmet. He was running at speed straight for the Emissary, slicing and chopping with the glowing sword.

The Prince could see something very strange and dark standing at the centre of a ring of tall warriors holding out lances. This at last was surely the Emissary. The thing stood nearly six feet tall and wore black armour, but the blackness was so total that it seemed to suck the light and air from everything around it. As if that little piece of the battlefield and the air above it were in some other realm.

Lissa called out from behind him, 'Be careful!' An

241

arrow flew past him and took out one of the lance holders, and then there was another, and another lance holder fell forwards. The Prince sprinted forward, charged with a mysterious burst of energy and a kind of inner certainty he would never have believed possible.

He struck out with the sword, hacking away at the porcupine of lances, slicing through the wood and then slicing through the honour guards that held them. Behind him Lissa finished off one after another with her arrows. They worked their way around the circle from both ends. The honour guards stayed in their defensive positions, pulling back as their colleagues fell dead, and forming themselves into a smaller and tighter circle around the Emissary.

'Poor Baku is dead,' Lissa called out. 'He died saving me.' And she spurred her horse around the circle, still firing arrows as she rode.

The howling sound of wolves rose up from somewhere on the edge of the battlefield, cutting through the cries and sounds of battle. The Prince knew then that when the day was done the wolves would have their pick, their feast among the vanquished. He remembered then waking and hearing them howl in exactly this way outside the old palace when Ayah woke him so roughly that morning.

One of the honour guards broke ranks and stepped forward. Lissa's horse stumbled over his lowered lance and pitched Lissa onto the ground. The Prince took the guard down at once with a single blow and helped

Lissa to her feet. She leaned against him, trembling, and together they looked across the thin ranks of the few remaining honour guards to the dark negative thing that was the Emissary.

Lissa had two arrows left and there were now just four honour guards standing together holding their lances out towards them. She fired her last two arrows rapidly, one after the other, aiming at the outer two guards who both fell at once in silence to the ground. The Prince lunged forward and attacked one of the remaining two, while the other guard went for Lissa at once with his lance. The Prince saw Lissa's dagger dashed from her hand and she stood awkwardly for a moment, unarmed, wounded and weak.

The Prince had no choice.

His love for Lissa overrode his sense of duty, overrode everything, and instinctively, without thought, he threw his sword, handle first, to Lissa. She caught it and also caught the Prince's eye and they looked at one another across the few yards of bloodied ground and the scattered bodies, and each felt a surge of love even as Lissa felt the strength of the sword rush through her arm and her whole body.

The Prince, completely unarmed, moved across the fallen bodies of the honour guard to stand in front of the Emissary.

Lissa attacked the remaining guard, the sword flashing and slicing the air like lightning.

243

Even as the last guard's body fell a sudden coldness swept across the plain. A storm of glittering ice particles swirled through the battling armies. The ice maiden descended with her full force on the whole battle and rendered the fighting impossible. Soldiers from both sides simply stopped, caught up in her sudden and frozen embrace. Each was invisible to the other, each warrior held in his own captive pocket of frozen, misted air and ice. All save for a small circle in the middle of the plain where the Emissary and the Prince stood facing one another.

CHAPTER TWENTY-EIGHT

The Emissary

Through the blacker-than-black, cross-hatched iron grille wrapped around his misshapen head, the Emissary studied the boy in front of him, the noble and pampered Prince Osamu.

The Prince was dressed in bloodstained winter clothes. They had once been of the finest Palace quality, now worn down to shreds and tatters. He was unarmed, apart from the helmet on his head, which was decorated by a pair of antlers. He was slight too and no warrior to look at, but, like his ancestors before him, once energized by the sword he could become unstoppable. The Emissary doubted there was the mark of a single wound on him.

The Emissary noted the sudden drop in temperature, the appearance on cue of the one fallen demon, the ice maiden, the lover of the mortal world and its defender. She had managed to halt the fighting, he saw, by girdling the warriors in canopies of ice. It was her attempt at levelling the playing field, he supposed, although such niceties were some way beneath his understanding or

245

comprehension. It meant that it was all between himself and the Prince now. One thing troubled him: why had the Prince discarded the sword? He had given it to the warrior girl beside him. When she was threatened he had effectively disarmed himself, why?

These thoughts flitted among the deep, dank caverns of his imagination while the Emissary stayed still, exactly where he was. The slaughtered bodies of the honour guard were piled up all around him, he could smell the iron in their spilled blood and further off were the misted ice clouds and the shadowy shapes of the stalled battle. He could see his horse with the dark canopy on top, its reins tied to a small cherry tree, one of the few natural vertical details on the plain. The top branches of the tree were already in blossom, little linked circlets of pale pink shone now in the oasis, the one circle of sunlight against the blue sky.

Emissary and Prince regarded one another. The Emissary spoke first—except that it wasn't really speaking at all as he had no palate or mouth in the conventional mortal sense, there was just a vestigial hole, a nightmare slot filled with dozens of grossly distorted and discoloured teeth. Images from inside the labyrinth of his mind, thoughts and notions could be assembled and couched in mortal language and then transferred when he willed it. And he willed it now, he would take great pleasure in destroying the Prince and then laying waste the earth, but first he would play with him. Just, he thought, as an

246

earthly cat plays with an earthly mouse, before tearing it apart.

'Lost weapon,' the Emissary implied with a mocking shriek.

'Not lost,' said the Prince, and he couldn't tell if he said it out loud or just thought it. 'It was freely given.'

The Emissary opened up one of the dank recesses of his mind, one of the deepest, darkest chambers. A chamber that would have been better encircled and cut off for ever with slabs of the thickest stone. He let the Prince see into the chamber, opened it up to him, only for a split second: the mortal mind can only take so much horror.

When the Prince saw inside the Emissary's mind he reeled backwards and threw his hands up in front of his face as if this might save him from seeing what had already been firmly planted so drastically and so suddenly in his head. No sword could have saved him from that vision. If not, what could?

'Fragment,' the Emissary shrieked. 'Much more, destroy you. Lost sword.'

The Prince was still recovering from the first image that the Emissary had sent. It was so horrible that it served to strengthen his resolve. He thought of Lissa, he filled his head with a memory of the pale nape of her neck and the way her heavy plait of dark hair bounced against it as she rode. He thought of her eyes, too, and of the green moss and lichen on the rock and how those

247

two colours rhymed together. He thought of the colour of the sky, of the many skies he had seen going back to his childhood, the glowing dawns and sunsets. He held them up in his mind, displayed them for the Emissary. It was his only way of fighting back against the horrors he had been sent. It was then that the Prince half-realized why he had been allowed to raise himself, to follow his instincts in the way that he had. Sequestered with his books and his pots, his music, poetry, beauty and the imagination, his tutors, wiser than he realized, knew that there were other ways of fighting and that the sword may not always be the answer.

The Prince was only half-conscious of these things, he was operating purely on instinct. He stared hard at the iron mask in front of him. He concentrated on the images in his own head. He ransacked his memory and his imagination, like a burglar racing through a treasure store. He held up a succession of beautiful things and moments in a feverish excitement and then quickly moved on to another treasure and another. He bombarded the Emissary with images of beauty and love.

The Emissary was puzzled and distracted. It was as if the Prince Osamu were attacking him directly somehow, his cavernous mind was suddenly filled with bright and mysterious images of the mortal world. He could make little or no sense of the profusion or the way these disparate images were meant to be understood; he couldn't see what the Prince was doing, but he found it hard to

248

fight back under the assault. He was so distracted that he did not notice the sudden lifting of the ice cloud as the ice maiden swept upwards again, as if on cue, releasing Lissa and all the other warriors back into the warmer air and light. Visibility returned and Lissa dispatched the final honour guard and made the leap of a few steps to be next to the Prince. He did not even turn to acknowledge her.

She moved her other hand across to grasp the sword handle with both hands, and with her own mind suddenly filled with the beauty of the cherry blossom against the freshly revealed blue sky, she raised the sword up so that it caught the weak sunlight with a flashing glare and brought it down again, hard, into the iron clad fold of darkness that stood in front of her and the Prince.

CHAPTER TWENTY-NINE

Wolves

The Prince Osamu came to with the howling of wolves close by. Lissa was cradling his head in her hands. It was a bright day and he found himself looking up into the gently waving blossom of a cherry tree. A big black farm horse stood quietly beside him, and scattered on the ground were shreds and tatters of a strange black cloth. It looked like the remnants of some very thick and recently burned curtains. A lance was stuck in the ground and a once-white banner flew from the shaft. It too looked shredded and as if it had been singed with a kind of hellish fire. Chunks of twisted black iron lay in various-sized lumps and pieces across the strip of ground too. Something horrible-looking seemed to be attached to or held inside the iron pieces. There were torn lumps and bits of greyish flesh, bloodied and scaly and with the suggestion of boils, pustules and lumps all over them, as if they were the mortal remains of something ailing and very sick.

The Prince remembered then with a start. He saw once more the horrible thing that the Emissary had allowed him to see inside its head. He stood quickly. The sword was on the ground next to him. He looked down at the blade, which was dulled now, old bronze or steel, rusted-looking, with hundreds of years of patina all over it once more. It was dripping chunks of hideous scaly skin.

'It's all right,' Lissa said. 'You managed to divert it somehow, and then I finished it. Together we killed the Emissary.'

'The Emissary,' he said quietly. 'I diverted it with thoughts of you, and the sky, and blossom, and water, and poetry,' he said, and he turned and looked out across the field of battle.

Smoke rose up from the field into the bright sunshine. There were hundreds of bodies scattered around and, beyond the bodies, in the wide and disciplined ranks of the hidden army, he could see Hiroshi, his appointed general, stepping proudly on his horse over the bloodied ground towards him, balancing a wide banner from his saddle. In front of him marched an old farmer holding up his scythe. As they walked the light seemed to follow them and the ground at their feet appeared suddenly greener, as if the ground itself were waking up and stretching after a long sleep.

'The comet has gone now, do you see?' Lissa said. 'There's just the sunlight now.'

'So it has,' the Prince said. He pulled the helmet from his head, and shook his hair. The helmet too had faded back to dulled rough bronze, and the antlers were just

251

that—no longer shining silver metal, just a pair of bone antlers, awkwardly slotted into the holes at either side.

Hiroshi dismounted and bowed before the Prince.

'Hiroshi reporting, Sire. The enemy is defeated on all sides. Many of the lowly mercenaries have surrendered. Our troops fought bravely. There were, of course, many losses, but not as many as I feared we might suffer. See how the very ground itself has woken from the cold. We will see a good spring now, and a fine summer, and later a good harvest for Kazuki and all of us who tend our beautiful land. There was help from other quarters, too, which you may or may not be aware of. Above all, Sire, you showed your courage. You fought bravely and the demon was destroyed.'

'In a single blow,' the Prince said, looking across at Lissa. She shook her head slightly from side to side as if telling him to say no more.

'Struck once and struck hard and true and with passion,' the Prince said.

'One blow or a million,' Hiroshi said. 'It is enough that the blow was struck and the demon was destroyed.' Hiroshi remained with his head bowed and then quietly drew attention to the hastily made stretcher that he was pulling behind his horse.

'I have the body of your companion here. The young man fell saving this girl,' he said, and nodded at Lissa.

Baku's body was draped over with a banner cloth where it lay on the struts of twisted pine branches.

252

'He shall have a hero's burial,' the Prince said, 'as shall all of the hidden army who fell defending our earthly paradise.'

General Hiroshi offered Prince Osamu his horse but the Prince demurred. He helped Lissa up into the saddle instead.

'I think I know the place where we might bury Baku,' Lissa said, bringing Baku's little map out from her tunic. She unfolded it and handed it to the Prince. 'This is where he buried his poor master under the snow, along with all those pots he was bringing to you,' she said.

'We shall find the place and do them both justice,' the Prince said. He thought about the pots, those lost pots. They could form the basis of my new collection, he thought, in my new palace.

The Prince pointed to the ground. 'These hideous remains, the horrible lumps and fragments of the Emissary, which lie in such stinking lumps all about us, must be burned.'

The old farmer Kazuki set to and a pyre was set. The iron and the flesh burned away with a greenish flame, and as they burned a hole opened up in the ground as if the plain were laid over a deep mine-working, and the fire and the smoking remains fell through into a deep hole and the ground closed over them.

They left the field of the dead. The Prince was at the front with Hiroshi and the farmer with his scythe, behind came Lissa on the horse, gently pulling the body of Baku back towards the forest. The remains of the hidden army sang quietly or applauded as they passed by.

The sledge dog appeared from among the ranks unscathed. The Prince ruffled his head and ears, and for the first time a tear came to his eye, as he pulled the faithful dog to him and embraced him.

'I knew it,' Lissa said, 'you love that dog.'

Later the hidden army carried their dead away with them on litters or in carts. The army of invasion were all left where they had fallen, either frozen by the ice maiden or struck down in battle. It was not long before a pack of wolves were among them making short work of the corpses.

Over the following days and weeks the hidden army faded back into the land, took themselves back to their farms and their peaceful towns and villages. Hiroshi offered to take charge of the sword and the helmet.

'I will, of course, find a suitable guardian for each of these pieces,' he said. 'They will be scattered widely as before, a craftsman or a farmer or an apprentice will hold them, and they will be held until such time as whichever of your descendants needs them. And then a way will be found to bring them together.'

'Not for a long time I hope,' the Prince said.

'Not for a very long time, I am sure,' the General said.

Old Kazuki with the keen-bladed scythe had studied Baku's sketch map and offered to take Lissa and the Prince on their journey with the remains of Baku.

'I know the area along the river, I know all the ferry-men. I am sure that we can find the place.'

CHAPTER THIRTY

The Summer at the River

Lissa's leg healed. She suffered no lasting injury from the wound, and there was almost no scar. Since the winter the Prince, Lissa, and the sledge dog had been at Hiroshi's estate. The Prince had written several poems about Lissa. Indeed, it seemed that she had renewed and deepened his vision and he had written most of them excitedly at night while she slept with the dog curled at his feet. The poems were inscribed in fine brush calligraphy on sheets of vellum while moths bumped against the bright lamp on the lacquered desk. He planned to have the poems bound into books later so that their future children might read them.

They had travelled slowly across the land and through the spring together. Baku's body had been cremated on one of the many pyres for fallen heroes. Some of his ashes were contained in the little cobalt glazed pot that Baku had brought with him on his own journey from the river during the harsh winter before. The rest of his remains were in an old glazed water pot taken from the house that they had all so recently taken refuge in: it seemed right somehow. The Prince and Lissa rode side by side at all times. Kazuki rode ahead of them, and he kept his sharpened scythe strapped to the saddle.

The Prince would look over at Lissa in wonder every so often as they rode together. It was early summer and she wore a long white cotton shift dress, made of a filmy, almost transparent fabric, belted at the waist and buttoned tight at the neck, and she wore a broad-brimmed black sun hat in finely woven straw. Her plait, her twisted river of dark hair, hung down heavily below the brim of the hat and bounced against the nape of her neck as she rode, in just the way he had first noticed. It was one of the very images, the weight and tenderness of that hair against that neck, that he had allowed to fill his mind as he had stood facing the horror of the iron-clad Emissary on that cold field of battle in what seemed a lifetime ago.

Once they reached the river Kazuki asked questions of the people they saw working at or on the water. One fish-erman came ashore excitedly; he recognized the Prince.

'I fought for you, for us,' he said. 'This has been a place of wonders since that battle.'

'How so?' Kazuki asked.

'Near the ferryman, a league or so upriver, there is a mound of snow and ice. It does not melt in the sun. She has left it there.'

'She?' the Prince said.

'The ice maiden,' the fisherman said. 'The one who froze the battlefield. She put it there.'

'I thought I saw something once,' Lissa said. 'A swirl of ice and snow, yet I thought it had the form of a woman. I went down on my knees, head bowed, I knew I should not look at her.'

There was a time when the Prince would have made a quick cynical and barbed comment about such old superstitious beliefs, but not now.

'Could you show us the place?' he said.

'Of course, Sire.'

Beyond a wide bend in the river, past the rocks, the water narrowed and there was a ferry crossing. A wooden hut stood at the land end of a jetty and a little way from it there was a white mound under a stand of pine trees. As they approached the mound they could see that tributes had been left along its edge. There were little bunches of wild flowers tied with straw, candles, and slips of paper with names brushed onto them. They dismounted and the dog went and drank from the calm water beside the jetty. It was a warm afternoon. The white mound was dappled with rippling blue shadows as the branches moved in the breeze. The Prince knelt by the mound and reached his hand out. It was cold to the touch and powder-soft, like a fresh fall of snow.

258

Kazuki was already on his knees muttering a quiet prayer.

The door of the hut opened and the ferryman came out and walked over to them.

'Pilgrims,' he said, 'more pilgrims.'

The Prince turned to him and said, 'Do many come here?'

'Word has spread of the miracle of the snow, and so they come.'

'There is someone buried here, and some things too,' the Prince said.

'No one can touch the snow, it will not be touched,' the ferryman said.

'I touched it,' the Prince said, and he reached forward again and put his hand into the soft snow.

'You are the first and only,' the ferryman said.

'This is Prince Osamu,' Lissa said.

'Then you alone are meant to touch it, Sire,' the ferryman replied, and went down on one knee beside Kazuki.

The Prince rolled up his sleeve and plunged his arm under the snow. He felt the outline of something hard. He pulled it up out of the coldness into the daylight. It was a bundle and it made a clinking noise as he set it down on the grass. He reached his hands in again further this time and felt the outline of a face. He withdrew his hand.

'Master Masumi is buried here and so shall Baku's remains be placed here too.' He went over to the saddle

259

bag and pulled out the small cobalt pot and the large water vessel.

He took both pots and pushed them deep under the snow one after the other.

'We lay Baku's mortal remains with his old master, and may his soul rest in peace through eternity. We thank him for his great courage and for his sacrifice.'

The Prince withdrew his hand and a fresh fall of snow fell from the clear summer sky and filled the hole his arm had made.

They drank green tea with the ferryman in his simple hut.

'I am blessed,' the ferryman said, 'to be so close to a miracle, to a proof of one of the gods' own presence here on earth, to be within walking distance of a place they have touched.'

'We are all blessed,' the Prince said, and he unwrapped the parcel of Masumi's pots, and marvelled at the simple beauty of them, still perfect, undamaged.

The ferryman looked at them and said, 'A bit simple for my taste. I like something brighter, with a nice pattern of flowers on it, or some gold.'

'These pots are *as* flowers in themselves,' the Prince said.

* * *

During the long summer twilight the Prince and Lissa sat together beside the river. Swallows darted under the trees and the sealed mound of snow and ice glowed in the late light, perfect and intact again. The Prince had made a very neat little folded paper boat and he placed a shallow circular candle inside it. Lissa lit the candle and together they set the boat onto the calm water.

'For Baku, and for Ayah, my mother, too,' Lissa said, and gave the paper vessel a little push so that it floated out into the current.

'Yes, for Baku and for Ayah, and everyone else,' the Prince said.

A little further downstream the ferryman and the farmer sat together sharing some rough wine and a clay pipe. They solemnly set their own paper craft off on to the water as the prince's vessel floated past.

Osamu and Lissa watched their vessel float out into the centre of the river where both fragile craft were soon carried away along the stream. They watched the candle lights flicker and dance on the water until they were so far along the river that they became simple specks of light, like distant stars.

'Are you cold?' the Prince asked. 'I thought I felt you shiver then?'

'Yes, I am, I suppose, but then the fabric of my dress is thin and it is evening.'

'One day, some while before the battle, I sat out on a rock in the river, and I was thinking of your eyes.'

'Were you?'

'Yes, I was. I was trying to work out what I would liken the colour of your eyes to *if* I were writing one of my poems, which I wasn't.'

'Weren't you?'

'No. But if I had been I should have said that they were the colour of the softest moss on that same rock.'

'Would you?' Lissa said very quietly, her voice breaking a little as she spoke.

'Yes, my analogy was almost exactly right now that I look at them again.'

'Was it?' she said.

'Yes, the softest moss,' he repeated, pulling her against him. 'You are cold,' he said.

'You feel warm, though.'

Across the whole kingdom on that night others let loose their own little paper boats, and all with their candles lit. They all watched as the little craft drifted away on the waters. Some followed in their own boats, making it a celebration as they went. Every little paper boat, every glowing paper lantern was a soul, each one a brother or a sister, a father or a mother, a son or daughter, a grandfather or grandmother, a cousin, an aunt or an uncle, and among them were the fallen. The little boats sailed on until the light went out of the sky, or until the candle finally burned the delicate paper

262

structures and cleansing fire engulfed the little vessels, until there was nothing left to see but darkness and smoke on the water.

CHAPTER THIRTY-ONE

On Earth and in the Heavens Too

The early summer twilight soon faded down to darkness. Lissa and the Prince sat together on the jetty near the ferryman's hut. They were both dangling their legs down over the edge and dipping their feet into the cool water and gently swirling them about. The dog lay comfortably beside them and the Prince idly played with its ears or tickled its head.

'That poor dog needs a name,' Lissa said. 'We can't just call it Dog.'

'I think Dog is a perfectly respectable name,' the Prince said, suddenly using his old reedy and pompous voice. 'Isn't it, Dog?'

Lissa nudged him gently in the ribs. 'Not like that,' she said.

'How, then? Like this?' the Prince whispered low and slow and close in her ear, and then kissed the nape of her neck under the heavy plait of hair.

'Yes, that's much better,' Lissa said and then rested her head on his shoulder. They listened to the water tumbling over the rocks near the bend in the river. Crickets

264

and cicadas were chirping in echo. They heard bursts of convivial laughter from the hut behind them.

'What happens now?' Lissa said.

'After tonight we will travel together round and through the whole of the Hidden Kingdom, and we will establish a new place to live. Hiroshi confirmed that the old palace is now a burned-out ruin. We shall establish a new centre, an enlightened court.'

'And the Hidden Kingdom,' Lissa said, 'will do as it has always done—wait and train and be ready to fetch the helmet and the sword together whenever they are needed.'

They both shivered suddenly as a bitingly cold little flurry of wind crossed through from the edge of the forest. It swept past them and shivered the placid surface of the water into sudden choppy little wavelets.

The wind had visible form too, there were pale shapes in the summer darkness, and they swirled over the water like smoke and then went upwards into the warm air. Lissa and the Prince both saw them clearly for just an instant, and it was if there were suddenly two ghostly faces locked together in the mist, but as soon as the smiling faces were noticed they dissolved away again, it seemed into nothingness, into curving swirls and smoky abstractions. Neither the Prince nor Lissa could be really sure of what they had seen, but their hearts lifted in a sort of joy at what they might have seen, and they held each other a little tighter and

265

closer as the whirling cold shapes danced upwards into the sky.

For Baku now all was a dance, a warm and ecstatic dance, a dance for eternity up among the stars, out among the whirling planets in the very centre of the machinery of joy. He could gaze for eternity on the face of his beloved as they whirled and danced together. His bride of ice and wind had made him warm at last. He looked into her dark eyes as they danced, and he knew that at any moment and whenever he wished he could reach forward and kiss those blood-red lips and feel his soul warm right through, over and over, for ever.

The Rock in the River

It was the rock I noticed,
Ancient and mantled with green
A sentinel guarding our approach
Moss-covered, soft green at the edges
Green like your eyes
How long had it stood
Surrounded by water
Vivid in its green coat
Waiting like me,
To be noticed?
To have your eyes
Of greenish water,
Your wood-nymph eyes
Turn towards me
With livid light
Dappling your shoulders
And your heavy plait of hair.
Your eyes were girdled then
With your own moss,
And with grass and leaves,
And thorns and resinous roses,
An attic flute played a sinuous melody
And in my listening dream
It was always an image
Of a girl like you

That I saw in that veiled inner space
Half-stage, half-wood,
With the melting summer sky,
A dappled figure, cool under the leaves.

The Prince Osamu to his bride, Lissa

IAN BECK was born in Hove on the Sussex coast in 1947. After seeing an exhibition of drawings for the *Radio Times*, he was fired with enthusiasm about illustration and becoming an illustrator. Be began attending Saturday morning painting classes at the nearby Brighton College of Art. Ian left school at fifteen and went immediately to Brighton to study art full-time. There he was taught by both Raymond Briggs and John Vernon Lord. He has since published over sixty books for children. One of Ian's titles, *Lost in the Snow,* was made into an animated film for TV, and his books have now sold over a million copies worldwide.